Nickel and Dime

Nickel
and
Dime

Gary
Soto

University of New Mexico Press
Albuquerque

First edition
Library of Congress Cataloging in Publication Data

Soto, Gary.
Nickel and dime / Gary Soto.
p.   cm.

ISBN 0-8263-2185-2 (alk. paper)
ISBN 0-8263-2186-0 (pbk. : alk. paper)
1. Oakland (Calif.) — Social life and customs Fiction.
2. Mexican American men — California — Oakland Fiction.
3. Mexican Americans — California — Oakland Fiction.
I. Title.
PS3569.072 N53 2000
813'.54 — dc21

An excerpt of the chapter "A Literary Life" was previously published in *Crab Orchard Review*, and is reprinted here with their permission.

This is a work of fiction. Any resemblance to any person, living or dead, is coincidental.

To Lillian Castillo-Speed, librarian extraordinaire

BOOKS BY GARY SOTO

Nickel and Dime
A Natural Man
Nerdlandia
Junior College
Novio Boy
Buried Onions
New and Selected Poems
Jesse
Pieces of the Heart
Home Course in Religion
A Summer Life
Who Will Know Us?
Lesser Evils
California Childhood
Small Faces
Living Up the Street
Black Hair
Where Sparrows Work Hard
The Tale of Sunlight
The Elements of San Joaquin

Contents

We Ain't Asking Much

For six years Roberto Silva had worked as a security guard at the Walnut Bank in Oakland, worked in close proximity to large amounts of money stained with the juices of life, torn and invisibly tainted with cocaine, marijuana, and God knows what other drugs. Roberto surmised that the money was dirty, or why would these greenbacks fly from hands so nervously? He added another theory. The lower denominations—fives and tens—gave off the peculiar odor of old men; still, he figured that the bills were worth more than the salt mines that gathered under his arms at the end of a workday. He lamented that the money belonged to other people, some of them feebleminded, sourpusses, income-tax cheats, or would-be killers in glossy red pumps. Some belonged to misers stingy even in offering a smile. That would have required a blast of energy, a minimum of six calories to lift up the corners of their mouths. Life's not fair, Roberto thought while he watched old Mr. Berger lean to his right side as he exited the bank. He was a regular customer whose colorful ties were wide as bibs. Roberto suspected that the old man's leaning posture was to counter the weight of money in his jacket's top left pocket; he could imagine no other reason.

Mr. Berger hurried past Roberto without a nod, a faint smile of recognition, or even an abrupt "excuse me." The old bugger rushed past within inches—no, a fraction of an inch, the width of an eyelash—of brushing against him. He risked a collision that would have proven that his awkward posture was indeed the result of hoarding twenties in his pocket.

"*Cabrón!*" Roberto thought, then admonished himself for this silent and uncharitable outburst. But the man should know better than to run down the people who guarded his money. Guarded it with their lives, mind you!

Roberto had spent the morning in front of the bank, pacing from the cement planter box to the iron bench along with Gus Hernandez, the other security guard, their steps grinding a path toward blithering boredom. Neither looked at the other for, as in a bad marriage, they had seen too much of each other in the course of years. Neither found the other worthy of comment.

Roberto fought the urge to plop himself on that bench. The corns on his little toes throbbed. His mind was dulled, lacking even one elementary thought to turn over like a shiny coin. Still, he had to keep pace with Gus.

He caught himself watching a dog the color of an old mop urinate on a parking meter. "This is stupid," he mumbled. It wasn't this beastly spectacle that bothered him, but his silent gambling whether the urine would slip over the curb in a sort of waterfall. The urine puddled impressively, but its mass was not large enough to create a flow over the edge.

During Roberto's tenure as a security guard, his countless yawns had permanently creased his face and stretched his lips until they were slack as a child's jump rope. At thirty-three he appeared older, somewhere in his early forties, his life more than half over, his stomach and precious innards still chugging along but losing speed.

This was how Roberto felt when the bank manager, Mr. Wallace, called him into his office, a cubicle adorned with snapshots of his family. Mr. Wallace's chair squeaked like a metal fart before the bank manager asked if Roberto would be willing to retire.

"Do I look that old?" Roberto asked, worried that perhaps he had indeed withered on the vine of life. He sat erect while asking the question. True, he had noticed that he left more hair on his pillow, that his front teeth, never really white, had yellowed like candles, and that actually—a pathetic admission—he had recently begun to use both hands to push himself out of his La-Z-Boy recliner. And true, unlike a great many tunnel-visioned oldsters, he had saved very little. He was banking that he would get married, sometime soon, and that he and this wife, whoever this delicate love might be, would care deeply for each other. At least for the first three or four years.

"No, *retire* is the wrong word." Mr. Wallace corrected his lax use of language. He explained that with the advent of better security—he pointed vaguely at the video cameras bolted to the four corners of the bank—one of the two security guards had to go. He employed the word *cost-effective*.

"But Gus is older than me," Roberto argued, his back slowly buckling to gravity and hurt though he strained to keep it straight, soldierly. After all, they were talking about his life.

The chair let out another metallic fart when Mr. Wallace opened the desk drawer and brought out a thick envelope. Roberto licked his lips and swallowed. He anticipated a packet of money. Instead Roberto watched with fascination as Mr. Wallace unfolded a form that, from all appearances, was in triplicate, possibly more.

"Yes, Gus is older," Mr. Wallace remarked. "And that's why we want to keep him." He bit the cap off his pen and for a moment let the cap remain in the corner of his mouth like a stogie.

Roberto blinked at his boss. He didn't understand.

Mr. Wallace leaned toward Roberto, a conspirator, and removed the cap from his mouth.

"You see, this job of yours is going nowhere," he whispered, then leaned back to wait for Roberto to size up the meaning. He waited longer than Mr. Wallace expected, who was prompted to say, "You don't want to be like Gus, do you?"

3

"What do you mean?" Roberto asked.

"I mean you have a future!" Mr. Wallace brayed as he leaned back, his hands now behind his head like a holdup victim.

I have a future? Roberto wondered. He had dropped out of Fremont High School when a classmate tried to crack a chair over his head, an act of violence precipitated by Roberto's refusal to share his answers during a history test that he failed miserably. After a series of jobs cutting lawns and hauling debris, he lucked into a job at a foundry in Oakland. First he pushed a time-whittled broom from one end of the factory to the other, and soon he was taught to operate a lathe. He would have kept on shaving metal rods into surgical tools thin as chopsticks except one afternoon at the lathe, a curl of metal shaving leaped into his mouth, the carpet of his tongue gargling the still-heated object. He remembered the struggle to cough up the shaving, his head bowed and his hand squeezing the tube of his own throat. But the shaving simply wiggled down his throat, momentarily lodging in his esophagus before settling in his stomach—all while the lathe continued to throw out a confetti of metal shavings. He remembered moaning, "Oh, God!" and a fellow worker slapping him on the back and shouting over the noise of the machines, "Throw it up! Cough it up!" But he had swallowed the shaving. When the incident was reported, Roberto was let go. The foreman didn't want to risk keeping a machinist who couldn't keep his mouth closed while doing his job.

But that was years ago. While nothing happened to him internally—Roberto feared his stomach might blossom open from the razorlike shaving—his life seemed to hang in delicate balance between one paycheck and the next. Now Mr. Wallace was saying that he had a future, an impression he had held about himself all along.

"Listen," Mr. Wallace said, his hands and arms coming down from behind his head. He looked furtively about the cubicle before he confessed in a near hiss, "I'm getting out, too." He divulged this news while gazing at his family of snapshots, teeth bared, though some might call it a smile. He then really smiled. "Roberto, get out while you're young! We'll pay you for a month, plus here's this packet of money as a gift of appreciation." His eyes cut to his desk drawer. With his teeth bared, he said with a chuckle, "You like money, don't you?"

That's how Roberto came to leave his job at the Walnut Bank.

Even before the prompting from Mr. Wallace, Roberto had thought of quitting. He couldn't imagine spending another year, let alone his life, up against the wall, his punishment for not cooperating with that thug in history class. He signed the forms. He shook Mr. Wallace's hand. The grip was nearly pressureless because, at heart, Mr. Wallace didn't care one way or another if Roberto dropped off the face of the earth.

Roberto spent the remainder of the day nearly prancing in front of the bank. He threw himself onto the comfort of the bench. He taunted Gus, a serious and loyal employee, one who raised the set of flags each day and more than once permitted tears to flood his eyes. For this really old fellow, the whip of flags was a solemn sight. Plus he took pride in protecting other people's money.

"*Carnal*, I'm outta here!" he told Gus when Gus asked why he was acting so sloppily. "I got a future. That's what Mr. Wallace said. So I'm getting the hell out!"

Gus's face darkened. He told him that he shouldn't use such language.

"Why?"

Gus's face darkened even further. "Because I'm asking you, hombre!"

Roberto abandoned his post—for who could fire him, now that the ink was dry?—and from a nearby pay phone, he called his friend Manny Sanchez, a mechanic in a transmission shop, the only guy he knew who had swallowed anything close to a metal shaving. His was a two-inch spring that popped off the shaft of a 1967 Chevy clutch and shot like a rubber band into his mouth. But this spring was less worrisome than Roberto's metal shaving because Manny's stomach was a globe-shaped beer belly that absorbed just about anything. He gulped the spring and kept working, though he did swallow numerous times to wash down the oily taste. Later he joked that he had more spring in his legs, having eaten one.

Roberto crowed that he was a free man. For a good time, he told Manny to get down to the bank, the sooner the better. "They're paying me good to get the hell out."

Manny arrived and the two left arm in arm, Roberto yelling that he was a free man and wasn't America great? He wiggled out of his security jacket and tossed it at Gus, who smoldered from this apparent desertion. He muttered in Spanish that Roberto was a low-class Chicano. If Roberto had glanced back that day, he would have seen the flags waving good-bye. But he didn't look back. The future lay ahead, just around the block. They headed off to a college bar with loud music and strata of cigarette smoke, a stink that made them feel belatedly educated, one of the crowd.

"I got it made, dude!" Roberto yelled over the music.

"That's right!" Manny agreed.

They ordered and ate a basket of fish-and-chips and argued heatedly whether or not the Pilgrims ate turkey at the first Thanksgiving. Manny was certain that those black-caped Pilgrims had dined on such a bird, but Roberto, drunker because he was smaller than his moose-headed friend, was in doubt. He was one hundred and ten percent positive that turkeys were from Mexico, his grandfather's homeland. How could turkeys walk all the way from Chihuahua to Plymouth Rock? Roberto asked. Dumb as they were, Roberto alleged, no turkey was going to walk two thousand or so miles to have its neck wrung.

"Prove it!" Manny taunted.

Roberto smiled, certain that Manny was cornered. After all, weren't they in a college bar? The students had to know something.

"Any of you know where turkeys come from?" Roberto yelled to the crowd, legs straddling the stool, a real buckaroo as he raised himself up, slipped, and sat right back down with a jolt.

The college students glanced at the pair and some hunched deeper into their bear-thick coats, fending off such an intellectual challenge since it was November and midterms were long past. The mind needed rest.

"I thought you guys were in college!" Roberto snarled when no one dared to scratch at this historical issue. He turned to Manny. "I say the Pilgrims ate acorns and shit the first year, and then maybe some turkeys later."

The bartender warned him to quiet down. And Roberto did because he liked the bar and intended to visit the place again, perhaps with a date. He had already prepared in his mind to tell this date—Marta, a cashier at Lucky Dog pet store, came to mind—that this was where he and Manny, a true buddy, had talked turkey. His face lit up with his little joke.

"I got no regular job," Roberto crowed, toasting his nearly full beer against the army of empties in front of him.

"That's good," Manny slurred. He raised his beer and set it back down.

"But I got willpower." Roberto pushed himself up from his stool when he said this but sat back down when the bartender knitted his eyebrows in his direction.

"That's important stuff to have," Manny agreed. "Willpower! Chicano power!"

The two laughed, drank more beer, and then released it in the men's room, where an exhaust fan stirred the air but couldn't discharge the stink out to the alley. After four wobbly excursions to the men's room, Manny had also decided to quit his job, snarling that no one except his mother could tell him what to do and she was dead. He got on the telephone and made a call to the transmission shop. He told them to take that job and shove it.

"Did you hear him, man!" Roberto screamed into the receiver after he wrestled the telephone from Manny. He handed the telephone back to Manny. "Tell 'em, man. Tell 'em where to shove it!"

Manny's lower lip fell open like a sack. He grinned for a moment before mumbling, "Grandma Moses's butt. That's where it goes."

Roberto was confused by this remark, but since his bud Manny had one more year of high school than him, he was convinced that it meant something.

"You got willpower," Roberto congratulated his friend after he hooked the telephone back onto its cradle. "Let me buy you an imported beer. Something from really far away."

They staggered to the bar but were told to leave. The bartender was tired of the two drunks, both unaware that their zippers were down. They departed without an argument. They took their happiness out into the street, pissing in wintry bushes forty feet from the bar and once again at the end of the block, like two dogs marking a trail for their later return.

At fifteen minutes to four, at the beginning of the 1990s, there was at least one job opening in Oakland. The job was filled that same day at seven minutes to six by a Samoan who could lift a transmission as easily as his lunch box packed with four sandwiches, a family-size bag of Cheetos, and a thermos of coffee laced with nondairy creamer.

A month later Manny returned to his job at a lower wage, a lesson in life because he was now engulfed in the shadow of the huge Samoan. As for Roberto, he held out for six months, watching television and living off his meager savings and a few odd jobs. These jobs let loose a reservoir of sweat he didn't know was inside him. As a security guard, he had used up his legs and part of his brain from boredom. But crawling on a pitched roof that summer and raising a hammer for eight hours, he discovered the horrors of real work. He hadn't known the body could take such punishment.

By late summer Roberto had to vacate his one-bedroom apartment after the electricity was cut off and the landlord began to bang on the front door as well as the back, shouting for him to get the hell out, that he wasn't playing anymore, that his brother-in-law was a cop who enjoyed breaking heads for sport. Roberto was poorer than the ants that marched darkly across the kitchen sink.

"I messed up," he confessed to his hands, which lay on the dining table like gavels in judgment of his unwise career move. If they had minds of their own, the hands would have clutched Roberto's throat and strangled him.

Roberto wiped his eyes. It was late afternoon, and darkness was coming into the unlit dining room where he sat. He felt more worthless than those straight ahead, no-bullshit ants, which at least knew their purpose. They could bed down in the ground while he, a man with a stone in each shoe, had to hike down a long road.

Roberto cursed his luck and scolded himself for believing Mr. Wallace's cheery talk about a future. In Mr. Wallace's world, destiny really existed. Early in their sabbatical from forty-hour work-weeks, he and Manny had talked about applying at Circuit City, an electronics store, both convinced that all that was required—aside from a clean criminal record—was a coat and tie. They hadn't figured on needing a high school diploma.

Having no job was one dilemma; finding a place to house his troubles was another. Roberto stayed at a friend's house for a few weeks during the summer but was asked to leave at the beginning of autumn. He lived with another friend for a week and then moved into a car whose engine just stopped while he was hauling cans to the recycler. Friendless, Roberto resorted to making a home of an abandoned Quonset hut in the middle of a vacant lot not far from a shopping mall. He moved there with his clothes, a few sticks of furniture, an ice chest, and a treasury of records from the 1970s—Santana, War, the Bee Gees, the Supremes, Grand Funk Railroad, Fleetwood Mac—timeless music that would outlast plutonium, it was so good.

He swatted a broom at the wooden floor, rounding up a cloud of dust that he prompted into a far corner, where the floorboards themselves were pinched nearly to dust by termites. With a swooping motion he wiped the hut's one window with an ancient newspaper and then sat down to consider its headlines. One headline said THE CHALLENGER EXPLODES! The astronauts were reduced to a human grit endlessly orbiting the earth. He sighed at this tragic news. And while he didn't wish to show those lost souls disrespect, he used the newspaper to close a hole in the wall where the wind whistled.

The third day he woke to the finger tap of rain on the metal roof. For a moment, confused, he thought he was bedded down inside a snare drum, the way the rain clanged. He dragged his hands down his face like a washcloth, his first cleaning for the day. He yawned, stretched until a bone in his back clicked, and sucked on a back molar pasted with crackers, a late snack from the night before. Roberto hadn't spoken to anyone in two days, and he opened and closed his mouth, for he had to keep those body parts of his working. He swabbed his mouth with his tongue in readiness for his first words of the day. He sighed and said, "Oh, God."

He stood up, sat back down, and glanced wearily at the cover of Santana's first album, a pen-and-ink drawing of a lion. Any other day, Roberto had surmised that the kingly beast was roaring, but now the lion appeared to be yawning. At him.

He slipped into his shoes, curled from rain and age, and walked in a circle, his one way of stoking a fire inside what a religious brother on the street called his God-given temple. A fire was what he needed—that and a cup of coffee laced with cream and perhaps a glazed doughnut or two would make things all right. He actually pursed his lips, the bud of his mouth deepening with lines.

"Oh, God, I need coffee," he said desperately.

Instead he drank water from a red-plaid-printed thermos and paced back and forth, admonishing himself because he could have done the same thing in front of the Walnut Bank and gotten paid for his time. But here on the edge of nowhere, he just raised a faint stink of dust as he toured the meager confines of his new lodgings. He found a pile of newspapers but was frightened to rifle through them, for the headlines might be even more unsavory than the *Challenger*'s explosion.

The window was rain beaded and foggy. He wiped the glass for a better view. He could stride in the direction of the new mall or chance the old commercial area of Fruitvale. It was a matter of a toss of a coin, nothing more.

Breakfast was a few moist crackers and a single tangerine. He risked stepping outside for his personal business behind a wind-whipped oleander and trotted briskly back into the Quonset, shuddering from the cold. He put on an extra sweater and scanned his home of two days, then left the hut, using a piece of cardboard as an umbrella. He trudged through the vacant lot, mud sucking his shoes, and headed toward East 14th and Fruitvale Avenue, the crossroads for Chinese, Vietnamese, and Latino immigrants. He knew life thrived among its bustle of merchants and shoppers but was clueless what to do once he got there. Still, he trusted that if he just mingled with others, shoulder to shoulder, his grin to theirs, his outlook would improve. If nothing else, he could pick up body heat from these people.

Lately he had begun to count his steps, one to a hundred and over again, an obsession that dried his lips from the repetition of numbers. But this morning when he found himself chattering numbers, his mind an adding machine gone haywire, he scolded himself to be quiet. He forced himself to turn his mind somewhere else. His vision fell on a faraway street where he noticed a car stalled in the intersection. Two men—worker ants—were pushing the vehicle to the side of the road.

"I wish I had a car," he said absently. He looked down at his shoes, two rodents moving through weeds and mud. "And a new pair of shoes."

He found his mind short circuiting, whirling with ideas and silly notions, images that, if held up to the world, would make little sense. He blamed his hunger, his lack of sleep, the high school thug who had nearly whacked him with that chair, and finally his years as a security guard, where his brain sought desperately for sustenance. His mind, he judged harshly, had become a large bowl of shapeless mush. And this mush inside his head demanded stirring. He promised himself that he would start reading books.

The rain stopped, and suddenly the sun broke through the clouds above the former Sears building, long abandoned. The jagged edges of its industrial-sized windows were lit with this new sunshine. The sun broke expansively in the east, bringing joy to Roberto that quickened his steps. He threw down his makeshift umbrella and leaped over a puddle, feeling that he was headed toward something good.

Walking among people further deepened his sense of joy. Some were herding children to school, and others were limping toward La Clinica de la Raza, a hospital. Others blew on plastic foam cups of coffee while they waited for the bus. He crossed the street at East 14th and halted in front of Alfredo's, a mom-and-pop market that took no chances—it sold both Mexican and Asian food, plus a few club-shaped ham hocks for its black clientele.

Raindrops leaked from the striped cloth awning over the storefront, one striking Roberto's knuckle, the sign of a blessing. He opened up his palms and gathered additional drops to wash his face.

The produce was set out in bins on the street. The shoppers pinched high-priced tomatoes and pears, held up paddles of nopales, peeked under the skirts of lettuce, and quizzed the mangoes with the press of their thumbs. While he didn't have a coin to speak of, he felt obligated to assess the produce. What harm would result? He sniffed a lemon, an acidic scent that was a meal itself, and inquired of a Salvadoran woman, over whom he towered like a banana tree, "The prices are going up, no?"

The woman was unresponsive to his friendly overture. Instead she continued to bag the lemons quickly, her hands the flittering hands of a factory worker moving without thought.

His stomach grumbled, and something seemed to fall off the inside of his ribs—the last of the taco he ate yesterday? The noisy stomach continued groaning for the food that was within reach; all Roberto had to do was pick up an apple and bring it to his mouth. I'm no thief, he thought, and scolded his stomach for tempting him to crime.

His attention returned to the short woman, now toying with peanuts. He suspected that she was ignoring him because she thought he was a street person without a single coin in his pocket. He tried again to establish a rapport with the woman because he understood from her, as well as others, that he was a mere apparition with no more substance than the glare on a windshield. "I said the prices are going up because of the frost." She raised her face—and said, "No speak English."

To this, Roberto, his spirit once again revived, remarked in Spanish that weren't the lemons a bargain and, hey, the jicama was overpriced but what a crunchy taste! The woman smiled the ruins of her teeth, which were trimmed in gold, cracked, and blue with shadows. Any other day, Roberto would have been shaken by this display, but today he was encouraged. If this woman could smile through the wreckage of her mouth, then there was hope.

He sniffed the produce, one piece at a time, and left when Alfredo, the owner, came out, wiping his hands on a red apron. Roberto didn't want to risk his relationship with this woman or Alfredo or the colorful flood of fruits and vegetables.

He walked three blocks to Sanborn Park, where he sat in the wickery shadows of a sycamore stripped of leaves. He rested his feet, but not for long. From across the lawn, a needle-thin junkie approached, twirling on a finger a sombrero gaffed from the wall of a Mexican restaurant.

"I got this hat here, my man," the junkie in bedroom slippers announced. "And I ain't asking much."

Roberto proceeded toward the library but saw that it was closed, though a light burned behind half-open blinds. He felt small in front of this ivy-shrouded building, small, suddenly weak, and almost delirious. He had a vision of the walls of the library opening and the books pouring out onto the street. He rubbed his eyes. He rubbed them until a light sparked behind their lids and a terror leaped upon him: he envisioned an avalanche of books smothering him with words and pure learning, dictionaries and encyclopedias belting him for his own good. He raised his hands as if in protection and let out a cry. He grimaced and sensed a burning in his stomach. The curl of metal shaving, rusted as a fishhook, about to surface after all these years? His face grayed to the color of river rock, and the latches of his knees buckled.

Two women approaching from the other direction gave him room on the sidewalk. They feared that he was drunk or, worse, another crazy on display. But within minutes, the pain in his stomach receded like the tide. He adjusted his coat, and in its improved fit, he felt a lot better.

The sun was now sucking up puddles and the river coursing

along twig-dammed gutters. The wind moved the litter along, and the people at the bus stop were gone. His happiness was all too brief. He meandered down Fruitvale and onto Foothill, a street that, except for the occasional upheaval of cracked sidewalks, was perfectly flat. He was baffled how a street could be called Foothill when there was no hill to speak of. Where were the fruits, too, as in Fruitvale? His mind speculated about a past when village life had the kindly locals eating right off the trees. Aeons ago, these locals wished for nothing more than what they could fit in their mouths.

He was prepared to return to Sanborn Park, where he could marshal these thoughts on a park bench, when his gaze made a roving turn. He spotted some Christmas trees on the side of a closed-up thrift shop. He paused and regarded this mysterious find, his hand massaging his stubbled chin. What are they doing there? he wondered. He walked past the thrift shop, stopped, and returned, his shoe kicking a pebble, for a second peek. They're abandoned, he surmised. Or why else would they be there?

Roberto scanned his surroundings, sizing up the feeble artistry of poor businesses and shabby houses dressing themselves for Christmas. Some storefronts were brightly lit with a lasso of Christmas tree lights, their windows white with the buildup of fake frost. Red bows hung in a black beauty parlor, and painted on the windows of one liquor store, a roly-poly snowman was tipping back a cold beer. On a distant roof, Santa and his sleigh were blown over but still pulsating a string of festive lights.

"It's my lucky day," he said to himself, and shuddered.

He approached the Christmas trees, glancing left and right, conscious of the gravel under his feet, and sidled up to them. He stood next to them, hands wrist deep in his pockets, and did his best to whistle. His whistling didn't last more than three seconds before the melody died, and he had to breathe deeply to get the song cooking again. He then faced the trees. If the trees had had

31792

hands, he would have shaken them. Instead he touched their limbs, his fondling hand exciting a scent of pine. He mustered up a scheme to peddle these three trees, each one shorter than the next, this family of trees, all orphans, two brothers and one sister. Yes, they're orphans, he agreed with himself, trees looking for cozy homes.

He hustled the two largest away, rushing wildly down Foothill while the rain-tipped branches slapped and scratched his cheek. He felt like a kidnapper, devious. He cut across Foothill onto 23rd Avenue and finally Ford Avenue, a cul-de-sac with older but tidy homes. The trees were heavy to carry without accidentally snapping a lower branch against the kick of his running knees. This took strength, and he had almost none. His breath flowered before him.

"I'm going to find you dudes a home," he said to the trees. "Then I'm going back and get your sister a place to stay."

He was convinced that he hadn't really stolen the trees but rescued them from oblivion. Time would whittle them to twigs and scattered needles, but before their earthly lives ended, he contended, wouldn't it be beautiful to be dressed up with bulbs and lights, Santas and candy canes, icing and popcorn needled on kite string? He cooed sweet words to the trees and, sufficiently rested, raised them up and continued. He walked halfway down the street, a dog bark prompting more than one curtain to part.

He halted to debate which house to try first. He ran a hand down his sweaty face, salted from his enterprising work. He caught his breath and climbed the steps of a house that appeared naked and in need of the Christmas spirit. He knocked lightly, then with gusto when no one answered.

A voice boomed like a gunshot, "Go away, fool!" and he didn't have to be asked twice and couldn't disagree with the man's appraisal of his scheme. To the hightailing Roberto, the voice belonged to someone at least eight feet tall with the girth of an ancient redwood. His next attempt was a neighboring house with tall black stairs. He knocked and the door opened immediately, albeit not wide. Behind the shadow of the screen door stood an elderly woman, small as a child. She was wearing a sweater and a housecoat and below those articles of clothing an apron with tidy creases.

She examined Roberto, who began his sales pitch brightly. "I got trees." He then remembered the line from the junkie with the sombrero. "And I ain't asking much."

She opened the door wider, a pot roast scent rushing the porch. Roberto's nose flared. His eyes widened and saliva bathed the buds of his tongue. He swallowed. This smell kicked Roberto's stomach into another painful mood swing.

"My husband died," the woman stated calmly. She unlatched the screen door and came out on the porch. "My children can go to hell. I never see them. Why do I need a tree?"

Roberto stepped back to give her room, swinging the trees away from her as he waltzed them against the porch rail. He was unsure what to make of the dead father and the children. He didn't know where to take his sales pitch. So he observed, "Everyone has a tree. Rich families often have two."

"The rich can go to hell. My children are rich, and do I see them?" The woman made this remark without an outburst or a gesture of flung-up-in-the-air hands. Her voice was flat. Her eyes were blue, their clearness suggesting more a child just learning her colors than someone who was at least seventy. And her face was like her apron, neatly creased.

"Ma'am, I need to sell these."

She measured Roberto's despair, her gaze first stopping at his shoes and then settling on his dirty knees. She didn't need to go higher.

"How about twelve dollars?" he asked.

She blinked at Roberto.

"They're special trees," Roberto tried. He remembered Manny drunk on the telephone. "They're Grandma Moses trees. You ever hear of that kind? They grow them in Portugal but also some here. In mountains we never heard of." He licked his lips, worried that he had done a half-assed job of describing the genus of the tree. When he started to add a historical touch by saying that Grandma Moses trees were popular with Democratic presidents, she told him to be quiet and went back into the house. He was set to drag the trees down the steps when she came out of the house.

"Where are you going?" She waved a coin purse at him.

The elderly woman bought a tree and invited Roberto in to help her string it with lights and hang a five-pointed star on top. The limbs sagged under the red bulbs.

"Go outside and look," she asked.

He did what he was told; after all, she was his first customer. He climbed down the black steps, rubbed his hands in the cold, and looked at the house for two minutes. On his return, he chirped, "Beautiful! The bulbs make it stand out. You can't go wrong with a Grandma Moses tree."

He sold the tree for six dollars and went away with a ham-and-cheese sandwich, the meat hanging like tongues from the corners of the bread. He devoured the sandwich while he carried the other tree in his free hand. He next tried Myrtle Street, which was less tidy; in fact, as he walked farther into the neighborhood, he realized it was junky. He was spooked as he passed dogs behind chain-link fences and saw a youth standing on a porch, a cigarette half hidden behind his cupped hand.

"What you got there?" the teenager asked. He wore a knit cap and baggy pants that hung from his hips. Any lower and the cops might haul him for in indecent exposure.

"A tree." He averted his eyes from the teenager.

"Yeah, like duh, motherfucker," the teenager sneered. Smoke

flowed from his nose and then was pulled back in, as though in his fierce nastiness he kept everything to himself.

"It's Christmas," Roberto said without missing a stride. The teenager took a bold step down the stairs. He let the smoke drift upward and real flames seemed to from flare his nose, flames from way down in the belly. The teenager continued to taunt Roberto, but Roberto didn't listen. He was going places.

The street was poor, but at the end of block he sold the tree to a woman named Peaches.

"That's a nice tree," she cried as she clapped her large and work-worn hands. Roberto could tell she meant it. He felt blessed to have such an enthusiastic customer.

Her husband was blind. Still, with his suspenders down and his slippers nearly off alligator-long feet, he followed Roberto and Peaches as they scavenged a closet in the hallway for the Christmas ornaments—four crosses of Jesus and some lights, alongside Bibles, broken candles, and hymnals almost as ancient as the Dead Sea Scrolls. The husband trailed them into the kitchen, where Peaches searched for replacements for the burned-out lights. He caught up with them when they returned to the overheated living room. His eyelids fluttered, and his mouth muttered something that might have been a prayer because he uttered the word, "Amen."

The husband hummed as the two fashioned a beautiful Christmas tree. When they finished, he asked Roberto in stutters if the tree was pretty.

"You should see it," Roberto chimed. He guided the old man's hand over the limbs as together they touched the bulbs, one by one, and on tiptoes a star shiny as a new spoon.

"Amen, I can see it!" the husband said, and Roberto caught himself saying amen for selling the tree for four dollars, mostly in change.

When he had left and crossed the street, Roberto broke into a jog. His pant pockets jingled like tambourines, the quarters slapping in time to his stride. They jingled the music of a man making a comeback in life.

Roberto fetched the little sister tree from the closed-up thrift shop and made a pilgrimage to Alfredo's market. He bought fruit, bottled water, and two hog-sized burritos, which he took back to his Quonset hut. It was nearly dark, and the sky was boiling with a new front of rain clouds. The threat of rain made people retreat into their homes, including Roberto.

He stood the tree in the corner and stripped off his two sweaters, then put one back on when his body began to cool from the long walk home.

"Your brothers got nice, cozy homes," Roberto informed the tree. "And you're going to have one too. A warm place for the holiday."

He ate his burritos and drank the water while remembering a previous Christmas when he was a boy in Texas. His aunt Virginia, snake mean, had prodded him and his cousins to visit Santa Claus at a department store. That's where her ex, Uncle Peter, worked as Santa, ho-hoing to the children. They were all brown skinned in that border town, where the sun had stained them the color of walnuts. Uncle Peter was five months behind on his alimony plus child support, though he had been seen driving one of the first air-conditioned cars in town. His aunt forced young Roberto, a sparrow of a child, to climb into Santa's lap on a Saturday morning when he should have been home watching cartoons. Roberto had just sat there, two fingers in mouth, scared not because it was his first visit with Santa, but because of what his aunt had told him to say. He recalled how Santa—Uncle Pete behind that beard—asked if he had been a good boy. He nodded and sucked harder on his fingers. When Santa pulled them out, Roberto shook his head and shoved back them back in like candies with their own natural sugar. When Santa asked what he would like for Christmas, he took his wet fingers out of his mouth and pointed to his aunt hiding near the Christmas tree. In a baby voice, he said, "Auntie says give her the money." He recalled how he was bumped from Santa's lap and Auntie jumped on her ex, pulling off his beard and scratching his face, tough as a leather baseball mitt, which was painted pink instead of its normal brown. While the two fought, Roberto reached under a chair for Santa's candies, a fistful, which his aunt let him keep because she was so proud of him. The department store ruckus even made the newspaper—"Santa slapped by former Mrs. Santa." Roberto shuddered at the childhood memory and drank his water.

The dark bullied itself into his abode, and he lit two candles. He admired the tree, fresher than he could ever expect to be. He got up from his cot and sniffed the needles.

"You smell good, little sister," he said. He pulled a needle from a limb and fit it into his mouth. "And you taste good, too!"

A profitable idea, rainlike, tapped him on the forehead. He could cut the tree down, strip its long and short limbs, and twist and bend them into wreaths, perhaps even brightened with ribbons and shiny things. His enterprising future stretched ahead. He took off his sweater, for his ambition produced an unnatural heat.

He took a knife, sawed through a lower limb, and bent it bow shaped. It sprang back like a car antenna. He took the knife up again and practiced on another limb. Some of the needles rained to the floor, but most survived, seemingly dedicated to his design. He cut another limb and then wove the three limbs into a halo-shaped wreath. With the limbs struggling to break apart, to snap back into their natural shape, he tied the entire prototype with wire. The limbs behaved and were newly transformed.

"You're looking nice," he cooed. He recalled how as a boy in Texas he had glued Popsicle sticks to a toilet roll in an effort to make a pencil holder. But the glue couldn't stand up to the summer heat and the Popsicle sticks came off; he ended up just trumpeting nonsense through the toilet roll until his mother told him to knock it off. Many years later, however, he was proving himself an artisan. There was definitely no heat in the Quonset hut to ruin his industry.

He hung the wreath on a nail on the wall and stepped back to admire his creation. It was good enough to adorn a door or a window or possibly the front of a car—he had seen a Volvo just a few days before with a wreath wired to the grille.

He twisted two wreaths and stripped off the small remaining limbs that would not bend. He had a use for them, too. He glowed over his handiwork, though he was saddened at the sight of what remained: a long torso of the Christmas tree nailed to a cross-shaped stand. It looked naked, nearly scandalous.

"Looks like you ain't going to get a home." His voice grieved for the sister tree.

It was scarcely light when Roberto woke to hear a pigeon walking across the metal roof, a grating sound that worked on his nerves. He read an old newspaper until it was time for the stores to open. He ventured forth with his three wreaths hooked on his right arm and a few of the short limbs in the crook of his left arm. On East 14th, he made his way to a variety store that he had spotted a week before. Like Alfredo's, the store sported a striped awning. But unlike Alfredo's, the place was empty of customers, a single bulb announcing to the public that the shop was open. A tiny bell chimed on the doorknob when Roberto pushed open the door, which stuck from the cold weather. He entered after wiping his shoes on a straw mat, for they had picked up enough mud to grow tomatoes. He scanned the hodgepodge of goods in the store. There were galvanized buckets and dread-locked mops, buttons and pins, chrome toasters and heating pads, aprons with forty-eight states— stuff that had more chance of moving from an earthquake tremor than actual customers. Time and commerce had stopped, and

Roberto was persuaded that he was in the right place. He could get a good deal.

"You got any ribbon?" Roberto called as he advanced toward the owner, whose eyes were large, luminous, and wet. He was seated behind a glass counter filled with packets of cheap screwdrivers and questionable batteries.

The owner, unfolding his hands, asked, "What for?"

Roberto was baffled by the question, but he remained committed to his simple cause. "I'm selling these wreaths."

The man's attention fell to the wreaths on Roberto's arm before he asked, "What color?"

"Christmas color," Roberto sang, now getting somewhere. "Red. A spool of red."

The owner disappeared behind a curtain door and reported back with a single spool. He held it up like a chalice.

"But that's pink," Roberto argued.

"Red." The owner showed him the end of the spool, which was printed with Red. Made in America.

Roberto was certain that the spool of ribbon had been there since the variety store opened. He took the spool and examined it.

"It's faded," Roberto pointed out at last. This was the best he could argue.

"But it's still red," the owner mumbled, his mouth barely moving.

Roberto pinched his nose. He could see there was no arguing with this man, who hadn't caught up with the sixties, let alone the nineties. "So how much?"

"Two dollars for the spool."

Roberto rocked on his heels.

"But it's faded! You can see that, can't you?"

"It's still red. You stand by the wall over there and you'll think it's red." The owner's hand shooed him away. "Go stand over there and see."

Roberto was tempted to follow the owner's instruction, but he stood his ground, pondering the price of the spool. In fact, both men were pondering the spool when a drop of what appeared to be water fell on the glass counter. Roberto winced at the drop, then raised his gaze toward the ceiling. His stare was so high, his mouth fell open. He leveled his aim on the owner, who appeared older than Roberto had first suspected—age spots overwhelmed his hands and face, and his chest had collapsed. The drop had fallen from one of the old man's eyes, and his sadness swayed Roberto. Two dollars didn't seem like too much for a spool of faded ribbon.

He paid and left with the roll of pinkish ribbon. On the street he unraveled a portion and was happy to discover that the ribbon was redder inside. He chewed off a length of pale ribbon and spit it in the air.

On a bench at Sanborn Park he wove the ribbon among the branches of the first wreath. His work was clumsy, and he had to strip the ribbon from the wreath and start over. However, his perseverance paid off, and soon all three wreaths were dressed up. He next tied ribbon around the short sticks with the intention of selling them as "ornaments."

"You guys are looking good," he piped to the wreaths and Christmas ornaments propped up on the bench. He stepped back to admire his inspired production.

It was then the junkie with the sombrero materialized. This time, instead of slippers, he was plodding along sockless in brown shoes too big for his feet. His appearance was as disheveled as the day before, except he was more fully dressed.

"Hey, hombre, I'm selling this hat your kind of people like," the junkie said, then halted. "Hey, man, how come you got strings on those sticks? What you into?"

"They're ornaments," Roberto said.

"What you mean?"

Roberto gathered up the wreaths and ornaments in his arms, reluctantly explaining that Christmas wreaths were popular, and bounded away with the junkie begging to trade the sombrero for one of the wreaths.

"It'll look good on you, homeboy," the junkie claimed. He demonstrated by putting it on his own head. With the brim down near his eyes, his face was thrown into shadow.

But Roberto broke into a run and outran this lowlife sidekick, jogging to keep up, the sombrero jumping on his head.

Convinced that he had to get out of the barrio to the richer areas to sell the wreaths, he took a bus to Piedmont, where white people and Koreans lived in stately homes as tall and possibly as old as clipper ships. He got off at Grand Avenue and Holly, but not before he sold one of his ornaments for fifty cents to a woman walking with a cane. It'll look nice in your lapel, he told her. He poked the ornament into her buttonhole and crowed how pretty it looked against the backdrop of her red face. He sniffed the foresty scent of pine needles. "Smells good, too. Save you on perfume." He sold it while the bus driver had his eyes lifted to the mirror, watching Roberto's every move. The eyes were bloodshot, but stern. He was the sort of large man who ate his sandwiches in two bites.

Roberto was excited by the two quarters joining the loose change in his pocket. Walking briskly, he could hear his success in the form of jingling money. He slapped his thigh and the money rang out like thunder.

He walked three blocks, smiling, but stopped his giddiness when a Piedmont police cruiser slowed to a crawl. The cruiser braked, its taillights glowing, sinister. Roberto was aware that the cop was sizing him up. Roberto's mouth went dry from fear. He and Manny had once been pushed around by these police, who had caught them peeing in a bush. They had pointed out that the bush was nearly dead, but that didn't stop the single cop with no witnesses from throwing them into the back of the cruiser.

First he bounced their heads off the hood. He complained that the hood was now dented and drove what he called their "sorry asses" out of the city limits. Piedmont was rich, and Roberto knew it was not to be played with.

He kept a nonchalant pace, and at last the cruiser drove away, trailing blue smoke.

"Shit," Roberto said under his breath. He heeded the cop's silent warning and kept walking.

He reached Magnolia Park, where he gathered small pinecones while sparrows hopped about his feet in search of fodder to keep them going through winter. He pocketed six cones. Shivering from the dewy rain falling from the tree, he hurried to a wooden bench the length of a coffin. There he tied a few of the cones onto the wreaths, happy with his floral touch. He gathered acorns under another tree. He pocketed a few and quarreled with a squirrel, well padded with fat and with a tail as tall as a bush.

"You can't have everything," he yelled at the squirrel. "Greedy *ratón*."

He couldn't tie the acorns to the ornaments, so he decided to offer them as bonuses with each sale. He departed, leaving the squirrel still chattering.

The climb to the richer homes of Piedmont was steep. His legs burned, his nose ran in the cold, and his breathing became shallow. The sky was gray as flint and looked ready to rain ice as sharp as flint. He was convinced that rich people dwelt in the hills because poor people couldn't climb there without either hurting themselves or using up so much energy that they just turned around in defeat.

He paused in front of a two-story colonial with a fat wreath in each of six leaded windows. He judged the wreaths hooked on his arms. They seemed like stuff raked from a gutter, and his confidence lost some of its air, an inner tube with a pinprick.

"Forget this house." He would have patted his wreaths to console them, except he feared that they might cough up a portion of their needles. They needed to remain full-bodied when he sold them, that or so pathetically naked that people would just throw him coins for trying. He had continued his excursion down the street when, by chance, a Volvo pulled into a driveway. He halted with his heart beating fast. It was now or never to parlay his crafts into bills and coins. He approached the man who was getting out of the Volvo. He was in his midthirties, quick to smile, and dressed in khakis and a windbreaker with leather moccasins. His hair was sandy, just starting to go gray. A second person got out of the Volvo; it was his son, a shock of very blond hair showing under his baseball cap.

"Sir," Roberto called.

The man stopped, a bag of groceries in his arms. He waited for Roberto to add to his one-word revelry.

"I think a wreath on your nice car there would . . . ," he started before his mouth stalled. His mind searched for a word, something as elegant as this neighborhood, something educated and appropriate. "Would . . . knock 'em dead." Immediately Roberto could have eaten one of the wreaths. His sales pitch had come out all wrong.

The man swung his groceries from one arm to the other, a sort of exercise, Roberto supposed, to build up his appetite for the goodies the bag held. Surely this man had to burn some calories.

"Let me see," the man requested.

By then the boy was next to Roberto, tiptoeing and eyeing the wreaths.

"How come he's selling sticks?" the boy asked. His eyes floated to his father's for an answer.

The father chuckled as his free arm snaked around his son's shoulders. His smirk burned up a few more calories.

"Those are ornaments," Roberto corrected the boy. His face flushed at the accurate description. He knew the boy, neither vicious nor snide, was calling them as he saw them.

The three eyeballed the selections until Roberto, suddenly brave beyond his own imagination, took the best one of the bunch and pressed it against the grill of the Volvo. A gust of engine heat warmed up his frosty mitts. Roberto was elated. If he didn't sell one, at least he might bring the circulation back into his hands.

"How does it look?"

The man smiled but didn't let his teeth show. He rummaged through his pocket, and for a minute Roberto thought he was looking for his wallet. Instead he brought out keys in a leather pouch that matched his leather moccasins. He triggered the car alarm, which sounded with a two-syllable chirp, and opened the door of his car for a package he had forgotten.

"Jason, go on," the father instructed, handing him the keys.

"Aw, come on, Dad," the boy cried. "Buy one."

"It's in style," Roberto said. He realized the depth of his mistake. No one in this neck of the rich woods followed the likes of Roberto. They led, and others followed lamely along, provided that they had the money or credit cards.

"Come on," the boy yammered again. "Mom'll like it!"

The father pulled down the bill of his son's cap.

So one was sold for six dollars, and Roberto wired it to the grill of the Volvo while the man disappeared to put away his groceries. By the time he returned, Roberto was done. His mitts were now heated up.

The boy watched, bent over, hands on his knees.

"You made these, huh?" the boy asked.

"Yeah, how'd you know?"

"They don't look new."

Roberto thought the kid was a wiseass but had to admit that

he was describing the wreath to a *T.* He liked the kid, who didn't back away from whatever made Roberto stink.

The father returned.

"So what do you think?" Roberto asked.

The dad offered a glance, nothing more. He paid with eight quarters and four one-dollar bills warm from his wallet. Roberto assumed that this Piedmont father nested on his butt all day, a rooster on a money egg. He assumed that he wouldn't want a free ornament or a bonus acorn. He had bought the wreath for his son, not for the beauty of Roberto's handiwork.

Roberto thanked the man, turned to go, then shuffled back and repeated his thanks with a "Merry Christmas." He was out of there within seconds, fearing that the father might cancel the whole order because the wreath was slightly off center and the needles were beginning to drop, drying on the prickly stem.

On the next block he wound his way up a curving flagstone walk. From the picture window, a grandfatherly man with a rolled newspaper in his hands snarled at him. Wrong house. He did an about-face and couldn't hurry down the path fast enough.

But at one brick house he was accepted with open arms when an elderly woman greeted him before he even knocked. She clapped at his presence and immediately beamed at the two wreaths on his arms and the bushel of ornaments.

"Ma'am," Roberto started.

"I know why you're here!" she sang. "It's Christmas!"

He was beckoned into the foyer of her large house but didn't dare take a step on the white carpet. The curtains were white and frilly, and the lamps on the maple end tables glowed without even being on.

"Come here," the woman called from the dining room.

"No, ma'am," Roberto said. "My shoes are dirty."

The woman considered them.

"You're a nice boy."

Her smile is too wide for an old lady, Roberto thought, and noticed that the buttons of her sweater were in the wrong holes. He also noticed that no one else was home, the refrigerator in the kitchen eating up most of the silence. Then an aged poodle, sporting a sweater, appeared. Its teeth were crooked and an oil-dark sludge leaked from its eyes. Roberto could tell the poodle, stuck-up little beast, didn't like him. Still, he chirped, "Hey, boy! Hey, girl!"

"That's Francis," the woman said as an introduction. "Come on over here."

He wasn't sure if the woman was talking to him or the dog. Neither moved. Then the dog turned, seemingly disgusted with the visitor. Roberto observed that the pucker of its asshole was dusted with talcum powder. The dog, Roberto knew, had smelled something primordial in the folds of his dirty clothes.

The woman repeated a third time, "Come over here."

Roberto grew scared. A transient such as he was didn't belong in an old woman's house. Nevertheless, he stepped out of his shoes when she insisted that he hang the wreaths in the dining room. A swamp smell hovered around his nose when he wiggled his toes. He hadn't bathed in a week, and with all his walking in rain and mud, the smell would have scared away a den of rats.

"*Chingado*," he muttered. To the woman, who had returned to clapping with excitement because she was going to see a wreath in her home, he called, "Ma'am, I got to go!"

But she pulled him into the dining room and forced him to prop the wreath on a cabinet with a glass front holding a treasure of wineglasses, pink-tinted champagne flutes, and Royal Copenhagen china. She forced him to rummage through a drawer for a hammer and nails. She forced him to raise that hammer and spike that nail into a wall. He hung his last wreath, which had now begun to rain a sizable portion of its needles. And finally she forced him to stand his ornaments in a vase of water. The vase was cut crystal, heavy.

"These are dead sticks, ma'am," Roberto argued. "They don't belong in water!"

In the vase, the ribbons were bleeding their pinkish dye.

"Robin, they're beautiful."

"No, my name is Roberto," he corrected. Immediately he realized the folly of giving his name away. Maybe she didn't hear, he thought, and hooking a thumb at himself, said, "Yeah, my name is Robin."

"That's my daughter's name. She's coming home soon. You want pea soup?" Again her smile was too wide and her clapping too loud.

Roberto knew there was something wrong with the elderly woman. Maybe she was demented or on the bottle. He would have liked a swig from whatever she was drinking, for his despair was deep as a river. He was scared, his bowels grumbling and suddenly loosening a fart that was forceful and not worth hiding. If he had been standing near the front window, the curtains would have moved.

"Excuse me. I didn't hear that," she said.

"My stomach, ma'am." He stepped back when he admitted his moment of disgrace. He could have taken the hammer and struck himself on the head to end his troubles. From the look of things, something was going to happen that would sink him to the bottom of the murky river. And no sooner did he think this than a car pulled up the driveway with the knocking noise of a diesel.

The woman paused, nose twitching, and inquired, "Do you smell something?"

"Ma'am, I got to leave." He wanted to snatch the wreaths from their places, but he controlled himself. It was not a time to hog his creations.

"Why? Have some soup with Robin."

There was no time for questions and answers, no time to pry a few dollars from this woman. Roberto was already at the front door, slipping into his shoes. As he worked them frantically onto his feet, the soles smudged the carpet black. He struggled to open the front door and scampered down the tall steps, just ahead of the woman. He saw from the corner of his eye the other woman closing the trunk of her Mercedes.

Shoes unlaced, he was down the steps and not looking back. As he raced to get away, coins jumped from his pocket. He stopped to pick up a quarter but saw the daughter—Robin was her name?— watching him. Mouth open, her face had a baffled look.

"Shit," he hissed.

He trotted two blocks, spilling coins that paved the already rich streets with more money. With his lungs speared from exhaustion, he slowed to a stop. One of his shoelaces was gone, torn off by the speed of his fleeing. He sat on a curb but stood up when a dog barked behind an ornate gate. Like Francis the poodle, this one also sported a sweater.

Roberto glimpsed over his shoulder a house whose lawn and flower beds were spiked with ADT security signs. Someone with a cellular phone was standing in the window.

"Nah, man, don't call the police," Roberto whined.

He strolled away, sweat bathing his face, and turned on Magnolia Street near the park in time to see a car approaching down the tree-lined street. At first he assumed the car had only one headlight centered in the middle of its grille. The car accelerated smoothly through the scattering leaves, its one eye growing bigger. But on closer scrutiny Roberto jumped, his fear shaking out more coins from his pockets. It was the Volvo with the wreath, and the wreath was on fire from the heat of the engine. The fire was eating at the needles, the ribbon, the pinecone, and Roberto's dream to make something of himself.

The smiling father tooted the horn, and the boy, cap turned backward, waved. Apparently neither of them was aware that the front of the car was on fire.

"Shit," Roberto repeated a second time in less than five minutes. He was never really one to cuss, but there was no other word to elaborate his fear. He repeated it for good measure and hustled away but stopped almost immediately when he heard a prolonged skid. The Volvo, turned profile, was in the middle of the street. A hurricane-shape funnel of smoke was rising from the hood.

In the distance a police car wailed, no doubt summoned by the daughter of the elderly woman with his two wreaths and the smudge of his shoeprints on a white carpet, evidence of a new scam going around like the flu. And the ruckus brought people out onto their porches, an unusual crisis in quiet Piedmont.

Roberto scurried away, losing an unlaced shoe as he banked around a corner. He stopped to gather the shoe but didn't stop to fit it onto his foot. He clopped along, a runaway mule from a circus. His circuitous route brought him to Magnolia Park, where he hid in the bushes. The sirens of the fire engines, now also getting into the action, howled. He lay in the bushes with his heart beating fast and sweat slowly cooling his poor and punished body.

He could hear the slow, leaf-crunching tires of a police cruiser making its rounds. He closed his eyes and saw only black behind his eyelids, nothing to dream about, until a light frisked the bushes and his eyes saw a bloodred color behind his eyelids. He realized that he was blood and bone and the cops wanted some, if not all, of it.

Twenty minutes passed before the cruiser left in a roar of exhaust. He rolled onto his belly under the bushes and, head lifted, crawled like an alligator from the growth of one bush to the next, determined to slither out of town if need be. He spotted two idling cruisers but kept crawling. He spotted the faraway lights of Oakland and could hear—was it possible? he wondered—a mariachi trumpet. Was it was playing taps for him or calling him home?

"How far do I crawl?" he asked himself. He patted his pockets. Most of the coins had fallen out. It took money to get into Piedmont, and ordinary people, like himself, had to leave it at the city limits. The rich intended to keep it all.

Thus, on his belly, Roberto made his way out of Piedmont.

Roberto stayed in his Quonset hut for two days, squabbling with the mice that had sniffed out his box of crackers. He risked only a brief departure to buy bottled water and a cheap takeout lunch of Chinese food. The sloshing rain erased his footsteps, and he was glad for the anonymity of his trekking. Still, in spite of his distance from Piedmont, he imagined his footprint exposed like an x ray on the white carpet, evidence to jail him for making poor wreaths. He could still see the Volvo on fire, though the rain if nothing else would certainly have extinguished it by now.

He had only been in trouble with the police twice: that time lashing the dead bush with his pee and once in Texas when he and a kid named Ralphie siphoned gas from the pumps. It was a Sunday. The gas station was closed, and while the pumps were locked, the hoses could be taken out of their cradles. So he and Ralphie emptied as much gas they could from those black, elephant-trunk hoses, each splashing a plentiful swallow of gas. There were six pumps, and altogether they nearly filled a gallon can. As they were leaving, a dusty patrol car stopped the boys. The cop got out and scolded them furiously, mentioning some of Roberto's no-good family members and dwelling at length on Uncle Jorge. Roberto argued that the gas was just left over in the hoses and therefore free. The cop shouted, "Free, my ass!" Stubborn Roberto said he was going to tell his uncle Jorge, and the cop, furious at this threat, exploded more fiercely than the gas can. He collared Roberto and shook him like a tree. Still, a sobbing Roberto swore that he was going to tell his uncle. The cop pushed Roberto, who staggered backward and fell to the ground. He cried but stopped when the cop raised him to his feet, twisted Roberto's arm behind his back, and shoved him on his way. Roberto ran halfway down the block, turned, and shouted, "I'm going to tell Uncle Jorge. You cow shit!" But he couldn't tell his uncle until ten years later. At the time, Uncle Jorge was bedding in a prison in Arizona.

He shuddered at this memory. He next considered the remains of sister tree's poor naked trunk nailed to a wooden stand. Fiercely he yanked off the stand and swung the trunk down on his bed. He recalled reading of such therapy, of a patient beating an object until he was cured of what ailed his heart. He whipped his bed, but it just brought up a cloud of dust, which made him sneeze for a few minutes. He threw the tree trunk—little sister—aside and read a magazine.

Roberto was reading when the walls began to vibrate. A helicopter? Tanks and mud-splashed jeeps all because of one lousy wreath that burned a Volvo? The window darkened for a moment, then flashed back to a dull gray. He stepped outside, prepared to raise his dirt-peppered hands or drop to his weak knees, a position that he had assumed regularly since he returned from Piedmont—prayer was one way of repairing a poor soul. But hovering in the sky near the coliseum was the Goodyear blimp. The Raiders were playing that weekend.

On Monday, when the sky was clear except for a renegade cloud stalled near the old Sears building, Roberto walked over to the library, for he had promised himself to beef up his brain. His pace was languid until he passed Sanborn Park, where the junkie with the sombrero reigned. Roberto picked up speed, though from the corner of his eye he scrutinized the area and saw only pigeons, the hoodlums of all parks, gathered by the monkey bars, their breathing harking up into the air.

The library was warm and well lit, and the atmosphere was

enlivened by the electrical juices of computers humming at the four terminals. It was a school day, so there were no kids, only a few mothers who rocked babies in their laps. Roberto noticed that one mother had a baby in her lap and beneath her clothes another in her belly. He acknowledged that Mexicans sure could make babies and happy and pretty ones to boot. This baby was singing, already a little mariachi.

The dictionaries were heavy as bricks and so thick that he was frightened by his puny vocabulary. At the table, he opened one to gaze at unfamiliar words that were like an altogether different language. He closed the dictionary and sat admiring the young woman reshelving books. He admired her because she was in her early twenties and intent on getting her job done. His imagination indulged his curiosity. He saw her as a college student with fairly good grades but not so smart as to scare away average-looking boys. He laughed then—to no one except the little freaky gentleman inside his own head—and said, "Oops!" He laughed because if he had her job, he would have coordinated the placement of the books by color. The blue books would go over there by the wall, and the red ones would go near the bank of windows. He would put the yellows near the bathroom and the mixed bag of colors would be placed by the computers. Thus, shoulders jerking, he laughed at the stupidity of his organization. His mind was delirious and swimming in his own silly notion of librarianship. He slapped his hand over his mouth to stop his giddiness. To become more serious, he turned to the rack of newspapers. He placed in his lap the *Oakland Tribune*, the Sunday edition. The weight was like a blanket over his legs. He propped the newspaper there, studied the headlines until his eyes adjusted to the small print, and then threw the newspaper into the air. He stood up, crying, "Ahhhhhhh!"

The librarian had been watching Roberto ever since he first entered with his cargo of street smells. She beaded a stare on his skimpy figure when he began to chuckle without control—another loony from the street? She furrowed her face with lines, mouth puckered as though from stashing pins there while sewing. She strode toward him and snapped, "If you're going to be disruptive, you'll have to leave. Understand?"

He nodded. He couldn't leave at that very moment.

"I'll behave," he said weakly.

When she had wheeled around and departed, he picked up the newspaper from the floor. He snapped the newspaper, coughed, and started to read the local news. What brought him to scream was the photograph of James K. Wallace, banker. He was found dead in a river in Yuba County with his pockets filled with twenty-dollar bills and some floating downstream. In Roberto's mind, the money was trying to get back to Oakland. The article said that he had apparently embezzled $39,000, possibly more, and had taken his life after a long-distance call to his wife. The photograph showed him wearing the same suit he had worn when, nine months earlier, he had confided in Roberto that he, too, was getting out. Roberto felt dizzy and his heart skipped. Roberto would never have translated Mr. Wallace speaking of "getting out" to mean the taking of his own life.

Roberto moaned at learning of this suicide, moaned and cursed, "*Chingado*," an outburst that he assumed was under his breath. But apparently the gust of that word was loud enough to echo off the walls. It deepened the librarian's dislike of him. She returned, pointed to the exit, and snapped, "Get out!"

"Can I have the newspaper?" he begged. He wanted to read the article once again and lick a thumb and rifle his way to the obituaries. Perhaps there were added details regarding Mr. Wallace's family or service.

"No, you can't! *Ándale!*" She stomped her foot, and her mouth puckered. Roberto could see how she might suck on needles on her days off.

Out on the street, he leaned his back against the sycamore in front of the library and prayed that the librarian would come stomping out, hurl a dictionary at him, and knock him silly with words he would never know. Knowledge sometimes hurt, as he had learned that morning. He turned and scraped a scab of bark from the tree and would have stood there, facing the tree, a bad boy who had used a bad word in a public place, except his mind turned a rusty gear. He decided to head off to his old employer, the Walnut Bank, and ask Gus why Mr. Wallace would have stolen such an amount only to drown himself without spending any of it. When Roberto fondled his pockets for change, he discovered a crushed dollar bill plus sixty-three cents.

"This is messed up," he declared to his open palm. A raindrop loosened and fell from the limb of the sycamore into his palm. Startled, he sent the nickels and dimes spilling onto the sidewalk. When he bent to pick them up, his fingers reached for a coin-shaped drop of rainwater. He tried to pick up the rain repeatedly.

He rode a squeaky bus to the Walnut Bank. He got off to stand momentarily in the black exhaust of an accelerating bus. When the smoke cleared, the air became sweet as candy and, as he learned quickly, was more promising than candy. Luck had placed him in front of a pastry shop. His stomach groaned, and if his hunger could have spoken syllables clearly, it would have shouted, "The peach pie! Get the peach pie, dude!" He swallowed a sour deluge of saliva. No, what sort of meal is that? Roberto wondered. He observed customers enter the pastry shop and exit carrying dainty white bags in their pudgy fingers. They don't need to eat, he told himself. He touched his belly and thought he felt the metal shaving, except it was a rib.

He punished himself by lingering in front of the pastry shop, sniffing freely like a dog. He tooted his happiness at the chocolate chip cookies and the carrot cake and appreciated highly the lemon custard in a plastic cup. He praised the sight of a tiered wedding cake with ropes of icing and the bride and groom knee-deep in frosting. Marriage looks so sweet, he mused.

Unable to stand the display of gleaming delicacies, he strode off to the Walnut Bank, where, as he suspected, Gus was standing with his hands behind his back, a captive to time. For Roberto, it was a homecoming. He was happy to see his old friend, so happy that his stride became an actual jog.

"Gus, *compa*," Roberto boomed.

Gus tilted his head at Roberto, baffled.

"It's me, *carnal*," Roberto boomed even louder. His joy was wild, and he would have given Gus a hug but knew the old man wasn't that kind of fellow, even if he was Mexican and *un abrazo* was loving affection between men, men and sometimes their animals—horse, dog, or squealing pig.

"Roberto?"

Roberto nodded. "I'm here to see you, you ol' goat, but also—"

Suddenly the glass door of the bank swung open. Mr. Berger emerged with his body leaning far to the right, the gravity of his dollars packed somewhere in his front pocket. Mr. Berger passed without a nod or a perfunctory smile. When he was out of view, Roberto continued. "I'm here because I read—"

Gus held a finger to his lips and shook his head. His heavy eyebrows knitted a shadow over his somber eyes.

"I know what you're going to say."

Gus stated that the embezzlement was a simple matter of greed. True, Mr. Wallace had stolen a large amount of money and perhaps could have gotten away with it, except guilt is a dog that follows you to the end. It took no more than thirty seconds to sum up Mr. Wallace's folly and another thirty seconds for Gus to kick a pebble between them. Silence followed; then, "Roberto, there is another matter."

Roberto scratched an ear, ready to listen. Gus breathed deeply and explained that the police had puzzled over Mr. Wallace's embezzlement and Roberto's departure—a sly connection between the two? There were also inquiries about Roberto's character.

"I spoke up for you," Gus said with his chest pushed out. He wanted Roberto to know that he had vouched for him but that there were others, back-stabbing tellers and the assistant bank manager, who painted a dark portrait of him. One of the tellers said that she had seen him unscrew the lid on a bottle of wine while on the job.

Roberto's jaw fell open, and his mind spun.

"Do I look like I got money?" Roberto pleaded after his dizziness planted him back in front of the bank. "Anyhow, I left a long time ago."

"I told the police that. I told them that you were a good man." Gus shuffled his feet, opened his wallet, and brought out two dollars. "Get something to eat."

Roberto took the money with a simple nod; the amount didn't encourage him to offer a hearty thank-you or a brotherly handshake. Plus he was confused, his mind once again dizzy. Why would the police think that he had the ability to walk out of a bank with money in his pocket? He could barely get his bimonthly paycheck out of the office, let alone stacks of tens and twenties.

"I'm getting out," Roberto said, then swallowed the last vapors of those words. Those were the words Mr. Wallace used that late morning many months before, and Roberto was now certain what he meant by them. So he tried: "I'm leaving. Why is this always happening to me?" He considered the last phrase, wondering why every piece of bad luck was reserved for him. It was god-awful living on the street, but being connected to a robbery?

"You be good," Gus suggested.

Roberto ignored the suggestion. His mood turned dark. "I can't even sit in the library without getting in trouble." He swallowed this pitiful fact and a fat helping of fear. "If the cops come looking, tell 'em I'm a nice guy. Tell 'em I look like shit and I couldn't possibly have money."

Roberto hustled back to the pastry shop, which he noticed was called Heavenly Delights. He sized up the pastries, some of them so dainty that perhaps they were concocted by angels. He had money to either take the bus back home or eat two dollars' worth of something sweet. With his tongue, he swabbed his teeth for a morsel of sustenance and, finding none, he shrugged and entered the pastry stop, which was indeed filled with the delights of heaven.

The morning pounded Oakland with rain that made lakes in the vacant lot where the Quonset hut sat. Roberto woke to this drumming and wondered if there was sufficient water to drown himself. Was there a river to float facedown in, like Mr. Wallace, a river to sweep him to oblivion? He wiped the window and peeked outside at the rain.

The acids of his stomach groped for something to latch onto, like an iota of bread, a peanut, a coin of carrot. Starving, he held up three fingers, the number of days since he had eaten something other than the three cookies from the pastry shop.

Roberto opted to head off to the transmission shop to see Manny, his one friend, his only hope to fatten his sides. He scheduled his arrival for the noon hour. He arrived at eleven-thirty. With time to kill, he entered a Big Hope thrift shop to look around and, if the opportunity presented itself, lounge in one of its chairs and warm up. The thrift shop was run by a Christian group, so when he was greeted with, "Hello, brother," he wasn't surprised and didn't argue about the familiar use of "brother." He nodded at the smiling black fellow ironing ties at the checkout counter.

He sniffed the air. The faint smell of soup perfumed the air, and this aroma kicked Roberto's stomach into a cage of growling animals. Just before he had left the Quonset hut, he'd devoured the last of the soggy crackers, which broke to pieces when he thrust his hand into the box. But they hardly counted as sustenance because most of the crackers just stuck to his teeth and wouldn't wash down to nourish his weakening body.

When the young man at the counter smiled, Roberto felt inclined to explain his presence. "Just looking. I need some new clothes." He fingered his collar. "This has just about had it."

He stepped down an aisle of white shirts, some of them so large that the sleeves touched the floor. A full-length mirror glinted at the end of the aisle. Like a gunslinger, Roberto walked slowly toward the mirror but stepped away from this showdown, for the figure that loomed in front of him was gray as a handful of ash. Roberto was disturbed by his sorry appearance.

"I look like shit," he whispered to himself.

But he was in the right place to alter his ragged appearance. He considered the coats and pants and rifled through the shoes, his own shoes having been beaten by rain, mud, and the crawl out of Piedmont. He intended to swipe a shoelace for his left shoe and would have except he was encircled by three workers. They appeared without warning, like smoke.

Roberto was astonished that they could read his mind. "I didn't do anything," Roberto remarked a bit too loudly. He was ready to plunge his hands into his pockets and turn them inside out. He had nothing to hide.

"We've all done something," said the young black man. His voice was like syrup. He had cropped hair and wore brown glasses that blended with his creamy brown skin.

"We're all sinners here together," said another, a baritone, his chest as huge as a tuba. A large, older man with his pants pulled up to his chest, he resembled Humpty-Dumpty. But unlike that eggshell of a folk character, this person was black and very real.

Roberto winced. The cryptic utterance "We're all sinners here together" didn't make sense even after it was repeated by the white person in the trio of religious brothers. It didn't make sense until he suddenly felt his hand being groped and saw the three of them closing their eyes, heads down, for a spur-of-the-moment prayer. Roberto, not knowing what to do since his other hand was captured by his brotherly neighbor, decided to close his eyes, too.

"How do you feel?" the black brother with the syrupy voice asked when the prayer ended.

Roberto blinked in the hazy light of the thrift shop. He surveyed the three smiling faces.

"I feel good."

They led him into the back room, filled with donations, mostly boxes of clothes but also chairs and sofas, televisions and computers from another era. There were also a few bicycles with flat tires and rust-pitted chrome handlebars.

"Go wash up, brother," said the white brother, who sported a crew cut and was skinny as a pitchfork. "We have a shower if you care to clean up." He hesitated, then confessed, "I was on the street for three years. Did everything against the Lord's wishes. Called him names I wouldn't call the devil." A hand fell on the seat of a bicycle. "And now this is where the Lord has sent me to fix such things."

Roberto blinked at this white brother. His shirtsleeves were rolled halfway up his arms, exposing a swirl of tattoos, some featuring skimpily clad women. The brother rolled down his sleeves and professed, "We can help you through God."

The syrupy-voiced brother sidled up to Roberto and said in a near whisper, "Let's clean up. Let's take a shower."

Roberto couldn't argue with the suggestion. But a conniving thought crept in. He could shower, jump out of the shower, and say with hair wet that he had forgotten something so important that he had to leave. He didn't know what excuse his mind would fumble with, but he would come up with a pretense by the time he toweled off. But Roberto's will melted like the bar of soap in his hands. The hot water was luxurious, the needlelike spray picking at the crust from his toes and the dark shadow of grime circling his neck and wrists. Reluctantly he turned off the shower when a voice called from outside the door. The call was a gentle call to hurry up.

In front of the fogged mirror, he was tempted to rub the soap on his fur-tartared teeth. But he just scrubbed his teeth with the up-and-down motion of a fingernail. After that, as he was stepping into his old clothes, so sour that he had to close his eyes as he fit a spindly leg into his underwear, a knock sounded on the door. It was like heaven knocking.

"Here are fresh clothes," the white brother said as he pushed open the door. He presented him with khakis fitted with a belt, a T-shirt, heavy wool socks, and Jockey underwear. The clothes were warm, having just been ironed, and folded as carefully as vestments.

"Thanks," Roberto said, touched. He asked the person's name.

"I'm Robert."

"We share the same name," Roberto remarked, letting that piece of dispatch hang in the air mysteriously. He added: "Roberto. That's me."

They shook hands, and Brother Robert closed the door behind him.

Roberto was beginning to like this place called Big Hope thrift shop. He dressed and came out of the bathroom, a new man with sweat beaded on his forehead from the hot shower, and was further outfitted with a reddish sweater and a coat. Shoes were handed him, and Roberto was surprised that these people knew his size.

"We know a lot about people," the syrupy-voiced brother piped. "And by the way, I'm Brother Marvin." Referring to the baritone brother, he said, "That's Brother Julius. And this here is—"

"Robert," Roberto interrupted. "We got the same name except I got an *o* on the end of mine."

Brother Marvin touched his chin. He clicked his fingers. "That makes you 'Roberto.'"

Roberto liked hearing his name from someone who was good. Lately no one had spoken his name, and if they had, the tone would have been a torturing scold.

He was fed chicken noodle soup, which he balanced on his knees as he ate on a wobbly stool by the sink. While the others returned, one by one, to the front of the store, he slurped those noodles with dice-sized chunks of chicken and broke apart saltine crackers. He licked his fingers; an hour ago, the notion of putting his grimy fingers into his mouth would have disgusted him, not to mention possibly laying him low with cholera or TB. But licking the tips of his fingers, he was proud of his own flesh.

Toward evening, six men and two women came into the thrift shop. They were all clean, electric with God—two had hair that was standing on end. From all appearances, they were outfitted from the very ranks of the used clothes that they had washed and ironed. Roberto greeted them with a "Hello, brother. Hello, sister." And they greeted him likewise.

There was a prayer group before dinner, then dinner of more chicken noodle soup ladled into mismatched bowls from the shelves in the store. But there was also a tray of sandwiches and as many potato chips as he could fit in his mouth. Afterward everyone competed to get to the sink and be the one to clean up. It was a playful moment; all shared the enthusiasm of putting out a little elbow grease to show their affection for God and one another.

"Out of my way. Let me in there!" Brother Julius bumped his large hips as he pushed his way between the others at the sink.

Roberto was scraping his bowl while he watched them fight over the honor of doing dishes. He considered the remains in another person's bowl but checked himself, as he was certain that there was a passage in the Bible that scolded street gluttons such as himself about slurping leftover chicken noodle soup.

When the dishes were done, there was a prayer in the kitchen and discussion about their sordid pasts. Some admitted being former drug addicts, while Brother Robert admitted his old racist mind-set—he rolled up his sleeves and showed Nazi insignia. He could have such hateful messages lasered, he explained, but was inclined to keep his tattoos as reminders of his past. "But I wash my hands of those days," Robert said, nearly crying. "What was in me was the devil." He gripped the skin on his wrists, distorting the tattoo of a grinning skull. "And the devil is sometimes white."

There were a lot of "amens" and "praise Jesuses."

Roberto was asked to witness.

"Like all of you, I've sinned," he began meekly as he rose to his feet.

"Speak up, brother," someone called.

Inwardly Roberto wished he could give back his new clothes and the hot food they piled on him. He didn't like talking about himself in such a naked manner.

"I didn't like my job because it was so boring," he began at last. He informed his friends that he had worked as a security guard at the Walnut Bank. He asked his friends if they knew the bank, but they all shook their heads. He licked his lips as he searched his mind for a sin to recant. He told them that one day when he was truly bored, he lowered himself to his haunches and thumbed ants to their oily deaths. He punished the ants for getting in his way, for making him feel small, for their dedication to doing what they were asked—genetically speaking—without complaint. Further, how dare they walk in front of him! How dare they mingle their simple shadows with his! He told them that ants were low creatures and they hurt when they bite. With one of the brothers yawning at his confession, Roberto picked up steam by saying that he once thought of robbing the bank and would have except he didn't have a gun or the nerve. When two others yawned, he used the word *fuck* twice in his storytelling, but no one lifted an eyebrow.

"What else, brother?" someone asked.

"Well, I had hate in my heart when this dude tried kill me with a chair." He recounted how he had failed to share history answers with a classmate in high school. He didn't tell these brothers and sisters that his answers were flat wrong and that he would have had the same results if he had left the entire test blank. He didn't know them that well.

Roberto was offered a cot in the loft near a window that leaked cold air. He slept uneasily with snoring men who rolled, mumbled, and gnashed their teeth all night. The next morning, he was assigned with Robert to pick up clothes and furniture in the van. The thrift shop was in the business of saving souls plus refurbishing goods, for idle hands were the first to pick up a bottle and drink, among other ghastly amusements.

But before they left, Roberto wanted to say hello to Manny, since the transmission shop was just two storefronts away. He left the thrift store and traveled not more than sixteen strides to the transmission shop. He heard the hiss of a welder, the metallic whine of a ratchet gun, and, behind those sounds, the tinkle of wrenches on metal. When the ratchet gun stopped, Roberto yelled, "Is Manny here?" The shop darkened when a Samoan showed his face and body. Not yet eight-thirty in the morning and his face was streaked with grease. There was even grease around his mouth, and Roberto believed the mighty fellow might have enjoyed lug nuts with his coffee. But he kept this bit of conjecture to himself.

"What do you want?" the Samoan asked.

"Is Manny here?" Roberto's voice was weak as tea, and he sensed his anemic stature next to the Samoan. So he asked again but louder, spreading his legs slightly apart.

The Samoan studied Roberto. Then he pointed vaguely at someone in the pit, arms up in the air as if he were trying to swim out of his miserable station in life, and sneered at Roberto while he proceeded to pick up a transmission with one hand and walk away with only the slightest suggestion that it was heavy. He carried it at his side like a bowling ball.

"Manny, it's me!" Roberto called into the pit that was hell itself, except there were no flames to roast his sorry plight.

"Roberto?" The whites of his eyes were the cleanest thing on Manny's grimy face. Manny hopped out of the pit, his hands bleeding transmission oil. He stepped toward Roberto as he wiped his hands. He asked, "What are you doing here?"

"Ain't you glad to see me?"

"I'm working."

"I came because I was going to ask you for *dinero*." He said this while rubbing his thumb and index finger together, the international sign of "I need money."

"Just like you."

Roberto didn't feel insulted. Already he could feel a religious spirit in his soul.

"But I don't have to." He paused and waited to see if Manny would ask, How come? When he didn't, he volunteered, "And you know why?"

Manny shook his head.

"I'm with the Big Hope thrift shop, and my brothers and sisters are going to save me. It doesn't take much to be saved. Three days, I think."

Manny looked over Roberto's shoulder at the thrift shop. "You're with those losers?"

Roberto would have argued over that piece of slander, except the Samoan returned and glared at Manny. "What the fuck is this? You're here to work, not to talk to bums." The Samoan eyed Roberto to see if he objected. The Samoan wasn't mad, just trying to chum up in his own way. Roberto knew better than to open his mouth and disagree with this description. Truth is, Roberto reflected, I am a bum, but he hoped not for long. Not with the help of my brothers and sisters of the Big Hope thrift shop.

"I'll see you around," Roberto told Manny. He left, taking steps that were longer than the ones that had gotten him there. When he turned for one last glance, he saw the Samoan lecturing Manny with a large tool in his hand. A second, more attentive inspection showed that it was a finger, not a wrench.

Roberto joined Robert in a white van idling roughly in the driveway on the side of the thrift shop.

"It takes a while to warm it up." Robert gunned the engine, booting up a load of black smoke.

They were scheduled to pick up clothes, kitchen utensils, and furniture on their morning run. The van stalled as they rolled down the curb. Robert pressed the gas pedal. "Lord, it's us, it's us, Lord," Robert chanted. He turned the ignition, and the motor sputtered alive and the exhaust pipe popped. Robert smiled at Roberto. "He's listening. And we have to listen, too."

Roberto didn't know what to make of the last pronouncement. How could he or Robert or anyone else listen to God if he never showed himself? Roberto didn't question Robert. He gazed out the window as the business section of Laurel Heights quickly became residential. He liked seeing nice houses, liked seeing roofs and lawns, imagining intact families that would break bread together in the evening. He liked that somehow he was moving in a better crowd. And while the van chugged along, the red traffic lights turned to green; nothing was going to stop their Christian duty. Their first pickup was at large white house with a yard carpeted with leaves from twin maple trees. The leaves were lifeless, the rain having bullied them into submission.

Roberto was sure that the donation would be large to match the size of the residence. Instead they picked up a single cardboard box of clothes and a wastebasket full of squares of frayed fabric, panty hose, and old *TV Guides*. The next stop had them hauling a small sofa smothered in cat fur. With Roberto shuffling in front and Robert in back, they loaded the sofa into the van. Both sneezed from the cat fur and told the other, "Bless you." They honked their noses using the fabric in the wastebasket.

The woman came out in her robe and pointed at two plastic bags. "Can you take those?"

Roberto marched over to the bags. When he lifted them, they rattled like cornflakes. They were light, not heavy with wool sweaters and men's suits. "What's in here?"

"Leaves. From my gardening."

"Oh, ma'am, we can't take them." Roberto set them back down.

The woman argued that she was giving them a good sofa of antique value, and what was the big deal about taking a few bags of leaves? Roberto turned to Robert for a sign. Robert nodded.

They drove off with a sofa, the bags of leaves, and a sneezing fit from the cat fur. The normal-sized homes of Oakland abruptly gave away to stately homes made of stone and bricks no wolf could blow over. They were two and three stories, and some were castle-like, spitting out rainwater from their gargoyles. A few homes were gated, but others were fringed with white picket fences, a come-back from the 1940s. Roberto noticed this shift to opulent living and gripped his seat when the van banked noisily around Magnolia Park. In the park, a few of the trees were strung with Christmas lights. Two mothers were jogging with their babies in designer strollers. And behind these mothers were Irish setters keeping pace.

"Where are we going next?" Roberto asked nervously. The drive brought back a childhood memory of his annual doctor's checkup at a cinder-block office on the edge of town. He remembered that if his mother turned right at First Street, that meant they were going home. If she turned left, it meant a visit to the doctor's office, where a penguin-shaped nurse in a white dress lay in wait with a tray of syringes. That and other embarrassing pokings with his underwear around his ankles.

The van turned left.

Again Roberto asked his brother.

"We're going to . . ." He peered at the clipboard. "We're going to a street called Frazier."

Roberto couldn't recall whether his last tramping through Piedmont had taken him to Frazier Street. But when he peeked out the window, fogged from Robert's Christian humming, he could swear that they were just passing the house where the father and son and burning Volvo dwelt. But the homes looked the same, well kept and with more imports than all of Europe. He closed his eyes and envisioned the Volvo with its single eyeball—his Christmas wreath!—on fire.

"What's wrong?" Robert asked.

Roberto pinched his nose. The brief deflation of his nostrils made him answer nasally. "I'm getting a cold."

But life had turned more serious than a cold when Robert, after consulting the address on his clipboard, braked suddenly, lodged the van into reverse, and backed up two houses. Gunning the engine, he pulled into a driveway.

"Oh, shit!" Roberto screamed.

Robert eyed Roberto.

"Brother?"

Roberto had heard how thieves characteristically return to the scene of their crimes. He had heard of this sort of blunder, even witnessed it in movies and movies made for TV. While he was no thief, he saw himself fitting the bill when the van came to a halt. The engine shook like a dog before it let out something like a sigh.

There was no mistake. It was the house where Roberto had nailed wreaths onto the wall, placed his "ornaments" in a vase, and left an incriminating shoe print smudge. It was the house where the dog in the sweater and powdered butt lived, far more comfortably than his own sort. It was the house where the old woman was senile, possibly an Alzheimer's case, and the daughter's name was Robin, a springtime name. Yes, he remembered her name and the moment when she pulled unexpectedly into the driveway, not unlike their own arrival. He remembered his shoelace had come undone and was eventually lost in his own terror-infused run for his life.

"You okay?" Robert asked. The engine shuddered one more time, like the dead shaking out their last quiver of tension. In the quiet, Robert touched Roberto's shoulders. "Don't worry, Roberto. Work is a foreign country. You just got to go visit it."

Roberto couldn't make sense of yet another cryptic utterance from his brother. Nor could he make sense of a startling sight— hands cupped around her face, the old woman peered into his window with her lips pressed like a starfish against the glass and her nose, sluglike, moistening the surface. Roberto's shoulders jumped at this sight. The lips peeled away, leaving the imprint of an old woman's kiss. She stepped away from the van and waved.

To Robert, he said shakily, "My cold is worse. Can I stay here? In the van?"

Robert looked at the clipboard.

"It says we got to move a desk and . . . a thing called an 'armory.'" He scratched his cheek, baffled. "How do you say that word, brother?"

Roberto leaned toward the clipboard. He studied the word and expressed his opinion. "Yeah, 'armory.' Just like it's written is how it sounds."

The word was *armoire,* and to Robert it sounded heavy, like armor or army or the army's armor. He had hurt his back two weeks before and didn't wish to repeat the experience.

"Come on," Robert said, opening his door. "Let's go get the armory thing."

Roberto sat with his worry for a moment before he opened his door and stepped out with his face lowered. He was immediately greeted by the old woman.

"You're back!" Her face was red from too much blush, and her hair was wildly teased. "Is that your brother?" she asked of Robert, who was already marching up the two-tiered steps. He hadn't seen the woman on the side of the van.

Roberto grinned hard. He couldn't think of anything to say except, "Pretend I was never here."

The woman smiled false teeth smeared with lipstick. "I like your brother."

"That's good. But can we pretend like I never saw you and you never saw me?" He grinned again.

"I like you and your brother," she answered. "Christmas is a nice time, but we don't have those beautiful wreaths. My daughter got rid of them."

"But we don't know each other."

"Oh, that's nice." She clapped and stabbed her hands wickedly into her hair.

With the old woman in tow, Roberto climbed the steps to Robert, who was at the top of the landing and already knocking on the front door. Robert regarded Roberto and the woman, baffled at the pair.

"Are you the woman of the house?" he asked.

She nodded. "I'm coming."

Robert helped her up the five steps, a StairMaster for the aged, a workout for anyone with a bad hip. When she reached the porch's landing, she marched until her feet were in line and stood at attention. Roberto thought she was going to salute. Instead she pulled her hair and blurted, "It hurts! Christ, it hurts!"

Robert looked at Roberto, who said, "She's, you know . . ."

The woman led the two inside the house, but not before Robert undid his shoes.

"Looks like they got a real white carpet," Robert said.

Roberto kicked off his shoes and followed the woman and Robert into the house. Shivering, he complained of a chill, of the rain and the cold weather ahead. He inspected the carpet. His shoe print was nowhere in sight. And when he walked into the dining area, the wreath on the cabinet was gone as well as the one on the wall. He went up to the wall and ran a hand down the unblemished wall. He searched for the vase that held his ornaments. It was gone, and so was the old woman, though her chatter carried into the dining room, where he and Robert stood. But she returned tugging her daughter Robin. The daughter was tall and as wide as the armoire they were scheduled to haul away. Her wrists jangled bracelets, handcuffs to Roberto's way of thinking. He saw himself in those cuffs and his head slamming against the hood of a police car. He saw himself bleeding.

"Here's that young man and his brother," the old woman cried happily with a clap. "Make me a wreath! Robin threw the others out."

Roberto smiled at the business of the wreath. But his stomach soured with worry when the old woman repeated that she wanted a wreath and would pull her hair until one was hung on the wall. Her hands jumped into her hair and she started to yank at the hair at her temples. The pulling distorted her eyes and twisted up her mouth.

Roberto backed up first one step, then another when the old woman screamed, "Make me a wreath!"

She sobbed as her hands came out of her hair like bats. A few strands floated to the carpet, where the dog sat, panting from just being alive in a crazy house.

The daughter told her mother to behave, to quit acting like a child. Her stare darted to Roberto. She placed her own hands on her hips, banging a music from her bracelets. Her suspicion showed up as a shiny flake of anger in her eyes.

Roberto backed up three more steps. He wheeled around, hurried to the front door for his shoes, and skipped in his socks down the steps, heedless as Robert called, "Brother, where are you going? We got the 'armory' to haul." On the leafy sidewalk, he didn't glance back. His survival was somewhere in front of him.

"Shit!" he said, the curse word that could explain all bleak moments. The rain patted his shoulders and frisked them for their small dents where the skin lay over the bone. When he put on the shoes, he discovered that they were Robert's, not his, far too big on his own feet. He couldn't run without their coming off.

"Shit," he repeated. He clopped down the street, nearly skidding on leaves and the branches the storm had brought down. He leaped over toys and trikes left on the sidewalk and waved at the few neighbors who thought he was out for a brave jog in the rain. He slowed to a stop after he distanced himself from the old woman's house. When he stopped, he found himself panting in front of the house where the Volvo family lived. There was now a new car without plates sitting in the driveway, rain beading up on its shine. Even from where Roberto stood, he could smell its leathery newness.

"Shit," he said for the third time in as many minutes when the father came out, skipping lightly, already beeping the car alarm on his new Volvo in the driveway. The father halted and locked a gaze on Roberto, who, like a rabbit in headlights, couldn't move.

"You should get a better job than making wreaths," he advised. He offered this bit of wisdom calmly, without spite for burning up his family car. Still, he reached into his pocket for his cellular phone, for advice was one thing and police action another.

There was no retort from Roberto. This was the best advice he had had in a long time. He stomped away in the sleds of his big shoes, and when he heard the wail of a police car, he was already jogging across Magnolia Park. He cut into some bushes and lay on his back, his side hurting either from exhaustion or that piece of metal shaving swallowed years ago. He lay appraising the misfortune that awaited him. It wasn't that Mr. Wallace, now buried, was responsible for his present stature, currently the height of a salamander as he hid in bushes. It wasn't the kid who tried to bring a chair down on his head. There was someone bigger pulling the strings. There was someone else, invisible as the wind, mighty as rock, cynical as a clown. There was some god who set him on his back and now had him rolling on his stomach in the rain.

"Oh, shit." He uttered this cry when he could breath again and the pain let go its grip on his side. His eyelashes dripped rain. The tip of his nose held a raindrop. His eyes jerked left and right. An alligator, a reptile from another, nastier time, he ventured out of the swampy ambiance of ferns and thorny bushes. He moved on elbows and knees, mud on his belly and rain on his back. He crawled out of Piedmont and back into Oakland, his familiar homeland.

The Quonset hut was surrounded by a bulldozer, three trucks remarkably clean despite their roll through the watery trenches of the vacant lot, and five burly men, two of them surveyors in orange vests. They told Roberto about a parking lot for the mall. He received this news with his body as muddy as a toad, and one of the surveyors, saddened by this sight, opened up his lunch box and brought out a thermos. He poured what remained of his coffee and offered a sandwich to go along with the drink. Roberto accepted these gifts and ate and drank while watching the men point in the four directions. One even jabbed a finger toward the sky—a takeover of heaven? Was the entire world being paved with malls? The men's consideration boosted his confidence, that and what ended up as his last meal of the day, which he ate standing up. He felt better. If malls expanded, the chances of his getting another job as a security guard increased.

Clouds rolled overhead, but no rain fell. Wind plucked at the matted grass and pushed at the litter. Roberto judged that his tramping toward immigrant Fruitvale and East 14th had been misdirected. He should have jumped over the fence and progressed toward the mall. After all, weren't the lights brighter there? Weren't the people better dressed and every other person white?

The man who had shared his sandwich and coffee told Roberto to leave by tomorrow morning. They were going to bulldoze the Quonset hut and start leveling the ground. When the men left, only the sound of wind through the cracks in the walls disturbed the night.

The next morning, Roberto changed into the clothes he had stashed for such a time. Dressed in an orange sweater and green pants, a warm if mismatched combination, he decided that in order to start over, to rekindle his life, he would sell his collection of vintage records plus the chairs that his mother had lent him (and thus ultimately given him) many years ago. They were old and black where working hands had gripped the back to pull them from the dining table. Wobbly now, the chairs had borne the weight of a lot of men and women.

"I'm out of here," he said to a mouse that had come out of the wall. The mouse chewed nervously at the floor, dust and splinters of wood its breakfast.

He hooked the chairs on his arm and, with his thirty-plus records, he kicked open the door and left the hut just as some of the men from the previous day were arriving. Roberto would have waved good-bye, but his arms were full. With big shoes flopping, he stepped over the rain puddles and set his mind on selling his wares—his last belongings—at Sanborn Park, where there was sidewalk traffic. He walked past the old Sears building and stopped for a moment in front of Goodwill. He stared at a truck whose back end was overflowing with clothes and furniture. He was disheartened at the sight; with such an abundance of goods, why would anyone buy from him? Still, he pressed ahead with his plan. He walked to Sanborn Park, praying the sombrero junkie would not be there. He stopped once to catch his breath and rest his arms where the weight of the chairs pressed into his flesh. He continued toward the park and was relieved when the junkie was nowhere in sight; just a few men lingered near the slide and swings, talking quietly, their occasional laughter sending up white bursts of their breathing.

Roberto displayed his goods, propping the albums on the chair and around its legs. The passersby spoke Spanish, and his selections of rock didn't mean anything except another obstacle to walk around. They walked past, far more taken with his orange sweater than his wares.

"*Se venden discos, sillas, discos y sillas!*" he yelled through his cupped hands, his words reaching halfway down the street, over the sound of car horns, crying babies in strollers, and the roar of accelerating buses. He stressed in Spanish that the records were classic and that the chairs were antiques. His shout was more like a scold. He attracted only a teenage boy rolling an ice cream cart, who parked next to Roberto. The two scrutinized each other, and when the boy finally said in Spanish, "I'll trade you an ice cream for a record," Roberto jumped at this exchange. He snagged a coconut Popsicle, and the boy took an old Kiss album. The boy chuckled; he said the rocker with his tongue sticking out nearly down to his chin was really funny.

"I'll trade you a *bad* Fleetwood Mac," Roberto suggested when he was not yet half done with his Popsicle.

"Who are they?" the boy asked as he stuck his hand inside the cover of a Supremes album. It looked as though he was trying to stick his hand down Diana Ross's sequined blouse.

Roberto employed the "bad" over and over and flogged the teenager by repeating that he hadn't really lived until he heard "Rhiannon." With that ventilation of reason and a quick lesson on how to pronounce "Rhiannon," he won a strawberry Popsicle just as he was finishing work on the coconut Popsicle. He wiped his fingers on his pants and ate.

The teenager rolled his cart away when he realized that Roberto wasn't going to attract customers. Still, Roberto remained faithful to his merchandising plan, especially when two older women asked him to remove the records from the chairs. They sat in the chairs, their bottoms nearly overflowing the sides. They smiled at each other, their teeth embedded with gold, and got up and traded places. They laughed at the spectacle of themselves sitting in kitchen chairs on the sidewalk.

"How much?" one finally asked after she dismounted the chair. She clutched her purse.

"*Diez dolares,*" Roberto said.

The woman made a face. She said it was too much, and who did he think he was to try to fool someone like her? She knew the costs of used things.

"*Mujer!*" he countered. He explained that they were his mother's chairs and if he sold them, he sold a piece of himself. He was giving his family history, and family was a hard thing to give away. The woman was unmoved. She proceeded to whittle the price to four dollars for both chairs. Soon after the two women left, the junkie with the sombrero appeared in shoes that were oversized, barely on his feet. He appeared to be shrinking; even his coat hung loosely on his body.

"Shit," Roberto said as he bent and started to gather his records.

"My man," the junkie called. He clopped over to Roberto with the sombrero pressed to his chest. "What you doing today?"

"Nothing."

"Couple a days ago you was selling goddamn leaves and shit." The junkie laughed and slapped the sombrero against his twig-thin thigh. "That's a good one. I never known your kind of people selling leaves. That a motherfuckin' scam!" He looked up toward the leafless sycamore that bore against the sky the outlines of three empty nests. He pointed. "I'm going to sell me some sticks myself, motherfucker!"

He cackled as Roberto tucked his records under his arm and started toward the rest room, his bladder full as a water bottle. The junkie followed for a few steps but stopped when someone by the swings called out to him. The person called him Sammy.

The rest room was dark and moist with the beastly breathings of overflowing toilets. Roberto did his best to aim at the urinal, but it was futile. He zipped up, left the rest room, and was walking down the cement toward the street when he saw a cop with one knee in Sammy the junkie's back. It was a raid. Other cops were searching the park—the druggies had scattered along with the pigeons and sparrows. Even the litter tried to move in the wind of the activity.

"Damn!" Roberto yelled. Immediately he wished that he hadn't cussed so loudly because a cop wheeled around and started toward him. Roberto considered hopping the fence that led to someone's backyard, but his best course, he judged from the bulky hustle of an immense cop, was just to be calm and seemingly uninvolved. He touched his fly to see if he was zipped and continued his stroll. After all, what had he done?

"You!" a cop called. "Get your ass over here!"

"Why?" Roberto had stopped, and his eyes picked up the commotion of other cops as they were rounding up druggies, winos, and those such as himself, the luckless. One cop had even collared a dog.

"Don't 'why' me, you bum!" The cop snorted his anger and started after Roberto, who hugged his records and cried that he didn't do anything except pee on the rest-room floor and he was sorry about that. The cop's belly jiggled under his shirt and, in spite of his bulk, after a zigzagging cat-and-mouse chase across the lawn, he brought Roberto down with a tackle. One of Roberto's shoes flew off and the albums skipped out of his arms—some of the discs jumped from the album covers and rolled on the sidewalk in their own attempt at a getaway. The cop pressed a knee into Roberto's back and brought both arms behind in a chicken wing. He clamped Roberto's spindly wrists in handcuffs.

"But I didn't do nothing," Roberto cried into the lawn. He wiggled a naked foot, aware that his shoe had kicked off during the race around the park.

The cop left to help subdue a cranked-up druggie, returned, sat Roberto up, and asked what *he* was on.

"I ain't on nothing but my two feet."

The cop laughed as he yanked him to his feet. "You're right about that."

"I need my shoe." Roberto looked frantically about, but it was nowhere in sight. He worried that it had been carried away by the dogs that had come out of the bushes. "I'm going to get a cold. And my records are ruined. I'm just trying to get a job like everybody else."

The cop laughed, picked up two album covers, and led him toward an idling cruiser. When he pressed the top of Roberto's head and shoved him in the back of the cruiser, he tossed the album covers as a follow-up, adding, "Here are your records. I hope they're better than the one downtown."

"I don't got no record!" Roberto fumed. When he turned to the person next to him, he jumped in his seat: he was paired off with Sammy the junkie, who was wearing his sombrero. The sombrero came down over his eyes.

"Shit!" Roberto cried.

"Now why you talk like that?" his new companion whispered. "This here cop is a motherfucker, and I seen him tear up people." Sammy laughed, stomped his shoes, and lowered his gaze on one of the album covers. "Now who is that white man?" He was staring at the muddy photo of Joe Cocker.

Roberto ignored the question. He gazed out his grimy window at the park, where a few people had gathered to watch their exodus. He saw the teenager with the ice cream cart gathering up the albums. He didn't blame him; he would have done the same.

"Now, I ain't into white music," Sammy started in Roberto's left ear. "But you ever listen to George Clinton? That brother be wiser than the president. And when he ain't wise, he's out there and crazy like you and me. You hear what I'm saying?"

"I ain't out there!" He turned a fierce face toward Sammy, and his brow touched the brim of the sombrero.

Sammy sparked. "What you mean? You think you better or something?" He smirked and stepped on the album cover. "You selling leaves and shit, and you think you ain't out there?" He laughed, and the sombrero jumped on his head. "You got only one shoe—what kind of man goes around walking like that in the street, except one who's out there?"

Roberto grumbled and pressed his shoulder against the door, as far as he could get from the scolding.

"And that orange you got on! What kinda people wear orange sweaters except those going off to jail, motherfucker!" His companion laughed. "And you say they ain't something wrong with you!" He stomped the Joe Cocker album cover."

Roberto grew sullen. He had to admit that perhaps he had gone wrong somewhere. He wiggled his toes to keep himself busy.

As the cruiser pulled away, Roberto took one last peek at Sanborn Park. All he wanted was to renew his life, and here he was sitting next to a person he had tried smartly to avoid. The cruiser gunned down the street and banked around a corner, the road chewing at the tires. Luck had it that they drove past the vacant lot where the Quonset hut was now rubble. Two men were stepping among the muddy ruins. A seagull was pecking at a brown bag.

The cruiser picked up speed, and soon they were on the 880 freeway.

"Listen, Officer," Sammy said, leaning toward the Plexiglas window that separated them. "Me and my man here ain't done nothing that you can call wrong. What's wrong with sitting in a park? Birds go there. We ain't hurt nobody but ourselves. Ain't that true?" He nudged Roberto, who nodded.

The cop's eyes filled the rearview mirror, then returned to the slow freeway traffic.

"Listen, my friend here got no shoe, plus nothing to brag about, really. We need to deal, Officer." He rolled his eyes toward his sombrero. "We need to establish what you call a rapport. You heard of the word? *Rapport* is French, and those kinda people know how to work things out."

Roberto was impressed with Sammy's vocabulary and command of history. Perhaps there was something to learn from his companion, something valuable to learn about negotiating with the law. And not to be kept quiet, he added to the fund of their sorry state: "Officer, I got no shoe and I'm cold and like Sammy says it's time to rapport." He purposely shivered and sucked up the moisture in his nose.

"Officer, the rapport between us poor lives and your good life is something to consider." Sammy nodded to his own pronouncement.

"Consider, huh?" the officer asked flatly.

Then Sammy smiled his terrible teeth at Roberto. They were getting somewhere. He turned his attention to the officer, who seemed attentive. "So I'm willing to sell this Mexican hat for real cheap. Look nice on a wall at home. You got a family, don't you, Officer?" He waited for the cop to raise his eyes and fill the rearview mirror. But instead of his eyes, his teeth appeared with what might have been a smile or a snarl.

"This hat is a antique," Sammy pronounced, and let that statement hang in the air before he added, "And I ain't asking much."

The cruiser pulled off the freeway in the direction of the police station. Neither Roberto nor Sammy would find out if they had reached a deal until they arrived, or if the teeth in the rearview mirror were a smile or a snarl.

"Yes, Officer," Roberto tried. He was pumped up with confidence and regretted not knowing Sammy earlier. "It's a really old sombrero that maybe my grandpa wore when he was on a horse and the police were on horses." He licked his lips, certain that he was reaching the officer's heart, that the art of bargaining was finally sinking in. He elbowed Sammy's ribs. His eyes glistened with hope. He wet his lips again and added, "And like my friend says, we ain't asking much."

Literary Life

Silver Mendez sat hunched before a cup of coffee, black and too hot to raise to his mouth, and considered the two kids banging the side of a candy machine in the poorly lit hallway. They cussed at the machine. They cussed and mumbled the name of the professor who had met Silver in the parking lot. He didn't know if their accusations about the professor's asshole status were true, but Silver was familiar with machines that gobbled coins and gave nothing in return but another lesson in life's rip-offs.

When Silver was a student at Bakersfield State College and about the age of the punk squirreling around on his knees, he had been employed part-time by a vending machine company, his route dedicated to bars and hotels. His job was to refill cigarette machines. The machines were serviced by a butcher who had lost his union job and, retooled at the local community college, redirected his talent into repairing such machines. Gone was the whacking motion of chopping beef into edible parts. Gone were the chickens with their thighs folded modestly onto yellow plastic foam containers. Silver knew vending machines, and he knew the kid wasn't about to get his two quarters back.

"This lousy college of ours sucks!" the kid yelled. His lanky arm, akimbo, was pushed halfway up the chute of the machine. "Even our candy machines are trying to rip us off."

His arm was stuck.

"Don't pull!" his friend warned. "You're going to cut it off and bleed all over the floor."

"I'm going to kill this machine," he threatened.

"It ain't got no feelings," his friend reasoned as he knelt next to him. "How you gonna kill it? Metal's a material exempt from the processes of life or death. Least that's what I remember from philosophy class."

"I don't give a shit!" the kid argued. "I'm going to gut this monster!" He slapped the face of the machine with his free hand.

Silver dared to raise the coffee cup to his lips. He sipped cautiously, the black liquid first touching the whiskers of his beard and then finally his pursed lips, which were pleated from years of drinking pots and pots of coffee. The temperature of the coffee was perfect, though the taste was bitter as pennies. He sipped a second and third time. He needed a rush because the drive in his Honda—no cruise, no air, no nothing—was long, tedious, and, at one stretch of freeway, dangerous when a cow wandered lamely off the shoulder onto the road.

He directed his attention to the kid whose arm was still caught in the machine. But he knew better than to get involved. For all he knew, he could help the kid and the machine would tip over and crush both of them. He didn't dare lose out on an easy gig.

"This bastard's got me!" the kid screamed from his knees. The experience appeared religious.

Not only did it want the kid's money, now it wanted his body. Silver seized upon an idea for a poem, which came only when he was happy or full in the belly. He hadn't experienced either a full belly or complete poems in several years. He couldn't think of the last poem he wrote that was publishable. A moment, however, was upon him. He reached inside his pocket for a pen and then the napkin before him.

"Machines grab our attention," he wrote. The words blotted,

but he knew what he meant. "They grab our attention / then our arms. / We are attached to the corporate world!"

But the inspiration relinquished its hold on his thoughts when a hand touched his shoulder, lightly but in a manner that reminded him of the cop who caught him poking a screwdriver in the lock of a parking meter in Berkeley. This hand, however, belonged to the professor who had invited him to the campus.

"It's time," Professor Mitchell said with a frown. His tone reminded Silver of an executioner: time for your hanging.

Silver was on campus to do a poetry reading. True, his last book had appeared six years ago and that book had received no more notices than the ones he put up on the bulletin board at La Peña Cultural Center and those mentioned over the airwaves at KFPA. True, he had published in a few literary magazines and was runner-up in two poetry contests no one had ever heard of. He had recited his poems at dozens of Chicano demonstrations and had been an invited guest on a number of panels involving Hispanics. He had a name in the 1970s. His name nowadays, however, was well known only to a few friends, who mostly stayed away, fearing that Silver would hit on them for money. Nevertheless, he was comfortable with himself, though he knew that he was disappearing into the category of once young poets. That his mustache was touched with gray hairs was evidence enough.

He had been invited to Lowell College, a liberal arts college north of Los Angeles in Simi Valley. He had never heard of the college, and the college, he suspected, had never heard of him, either. But they wanted a Hispanic poet and Silver came cheap— four hundred dollars, his share of the rent money back in Oakland. Being no fool, he accepted the offer and sent a typed bio and a black-and-white photo of himself at twenty-six. Now he was thirty-eight, rail thin, even to the point of appearing tubercular. His hair had lost its bounce. His eyes were wired with the permanent markings of bloodshot, lunatic red. He didn't resemble the person in the photo, but Silver figured that photos lied anyhow. Once he had seen a photo of a good-looking fiction writer on a dust jacket and was certain that this smiling writer projected honesty and warmth, plus a spiritual vocabulary similar to the rap that the Dalai Lama spouted. And he got excited when he had a chance to hear the author read at Cody's bookstore, so excited that he all but ran up the stairs and tripped over his shoes. But to his and everyone else's dismay, she was mean as a snake, both when she read her story about a man who stabbed a woman with a fork and when she paused to drink from the clear cup of water on the podium. As she swirled the water in her mouth, everyone in the audience assumed it would fly from her cheeks. But she swallowed. After the reading, Silver introduced himself as a poet. She snapped, "So what!"

His photo lied, too. But his lie was simply about his age; anyone who studied his youthful photo would know that he was the same person. His youth had been spent on god knows what, but unlike that goddess on the book jacket, he wasn't a mean bastard. He was just unlucky.

"The room's over here," Professor Mitchell said in a near moan. He coaxed him down the hall.

"What about the kid?" Silver asked.

The professor said that he was a troublemaker. He shouldn't worry about him.

The room where Silver was to read his poetry was nearly empty. Three Chicano kids were standing around, two girls and a guy, their backpacks still on their backs. They smiled at Silver as he approached.

"Hi!" Silver greeted them.

The kids introduced themselves and said that they were glad the *gavacho* college finally brought one of their own.

Silver was glad, too. He needed the four hundred bucks.

"But we can't stay," the tall girl said, rocking on her heels.

Silver nodded. He asked, *"Y porqué?"*

"We got this physiology test," she explained. She pulled her long, shiny hair behind her ears. For Silver, the ear was the best part of a woman, that and long hair, provided it was washed.

"Ah, that's too bad," he remarked. He paused before flirting, "And just think, I was going to read a poem especially for you."

The girl smiled, mouth slightly open. On the back of one of her molars was a wad of blue gum. Her breath seemed fresh.

"Oh, wow," the girl cried, particularly honored. She turned to her shorter friend and smiled, her reason nearly shot to hell because she flirted with not studying science in favor of words arranged in a snappy order. They could stay and hear this poet or go off and memorize the less poetically frequented body parts.

They left.

Silver shrugged at their departure and scanned the audience. The room was filling up. He began to like this place and admonished himself for complaining about the long drive, one that started at seven in the morning and ended at three-thirty, just before rush hour. It cost Silver a tank of gas to travel the nearly three hundred miles down I-5 to the Tehachapi Ridge, climb the steep mountains, and glide with his foot off the pedal into the San Fernando Valley, where the college was. During this time, he had eaten nothing more than three oranges, all plucked in the morning from the tree in his backyard duplex.

The professor rattled some papers in his hands and encouraged everyone to take their seats.

Silver stood on the side of the room, nodding to the rhythm of the first poem he was going to read: "Cha-cha Heaven." He pushed a hand into his canvas book bag. He brought out his first book, *Tigres en Armas*, and then shoved it back in favor of his second collection, *No Más, América*. He fanned the pages and a whiff of age hit him in the face. He sneezed from that brief wind.

"Let's take our seats." The professor raised his attention to the clock. It was already ten after four. He turned to Silver and asked, "You almost ready?"

Silver pouted angrily, clenched his fist, and growled, "*Simón.*"

He was getting into his Chicano groove and was ready to slap these students with some truths about America. But his eagerness faded when he noticed the kid whose arm had been caught in the vending machine enter the room. He had his lips wrapped around a Baby Ruth candy bar. His sidekick, a few steps behind him, was devouring a Butterfinger. A valuable chunk fell to the floor when he bit into that six-inch sugar rush.

The sight of the sweets made Silver's stomach growl; saliva gushed over his tongue, that appendage that spoke its own mind when he was drunk. He swallowed the deluge of saliva and stepped up toward the podium, an old music stand, after a two-sentence introduction.

Silver beamed at the students. It had been a while since he stood in front of such a group. When he placed his two books and a sheaf of poems on the music stand, the weight of his work made it slide down like an elevator.

"What the hell . . ." Silver hesitated.

A few laughed. One said, "See, nothing works here."

He raised the stand, but it slid down once again. He and the professor attempted to tighten the bucklelike latch, but it was broken. Out of luck, Silver placed his poems and book bag at his feet. He decided he had better get started or risk losing his audience. He turned to the thirty or so students. He washed his hands, flylike, and asked, "How are we feeling?"

A couple in the audience said, "Okay." The rest just stared at him.

"Do we really feel okay?" Silver asked. This was his usual modus operandi, in which he would lead them to the notion of happiness, which was like air—all around us, he reasoned, and ready to suck in. Again he asked how the students felt.

"I put two quarters in that machine," said the kid with the Baby Ruth. "Everything's fucked here. Like that dude over there said, 'Nothing works here!' Drinking fountains don't work. Got to go to the bathroom if you want water!"

The professor beaded his eyes at the student but didn't respond to his outburst, which had a few in the audience clapping in agreement.

"But that machine coughed up all these," the kid continued, clutching candy bars in both fists. He started tossing candies snagged from the machine. The faster students fished them out of the air; others, surprised, caught them in their laps. One or two of the candies hit the ground like hand grenades. They were quickly picked up, unwrapped, and jammed into mouths.

"Mr. Casson, did you steal them?" the professor asked.

The kid explained that the machine just started coughing up candies after he pulled his arm out. He held up his arm, red where it had gotten hooked. He paused before yelling at the professor, "You're in no position to call me a thief!"

"I didn't call you a thief," the professor retorted. "I asked if you had stolen them."

"Same thing!"

"No, there is a difference," the professor countered weakly.

"Yeah, then how come I got a C on my paper and Josh got a B and we copied from the same book!" He was standing up now, his mouthful of candy scenting the air with sugar.

The professor, slightly red in the face, turned to Silver. "I'm sorry for this interruption. We would love to hear your poetry."

A student yelled, "Yeah, let's hear your stuff."

"Yeah, let's get it on," Silver said. He wished the kid had tossed him a candy bar. He was nearly dizzy from not eating, and the

71

sugar would have spun some sense into him. He touched his stomach. His guts—liver, spleen, kidney—had room to move because
his shrunken stomach had the mass of a deflated condom. The
three oranges were not enough pulpy material to keep a liver from
expanding, however slightly, and calling for more space.

Silver faced the audience. He wanted to get this over with and
sell a few of his books from his book bag. And to do this, he had
to start reading. And instead of the funny poem "Cha-Cha Heaven,"
he opted for a serious tone.

"This first poem is called "Modern Chains." He explained that
they were all in invisible chains. He cast a glance at the poem,
then up at the audience, and wet his lips for the forty-eight-word
journey that made up the poem.

"WE ARE IN CHAINS," he boomed. "CHAINS on the ankles,
CHAINS on our wrists, CHAINS on our sexuality."

He hadn't read the poem in several years, and only now, at
Lowell College, in front of an audience eating candy bars, did
he realize the poem was no good. He wished the poem was over,
but he still had six more CHAINS to boom before he would
finally clench his fist and cry, "VIVA FREEDOM!"

He read twelve poems, then a rambling letter from a *pinto*—
a prisoner—and fielded questions.

"Sounds like you didn't have a good childhood," commented
a girl with a chrome knob on her tongue. She had to say this twice
because the ball kept getting in the way of her pronunciation.

The question hurt. It hurt because Silver had had a lousy childhood and had yet to write about it.

"My childhood," he started angrily, "is my business." Then he
stopped himself when he considered her as a potential book buyer.
"And it's your business as well." He confessed that his childhood
wasn't brie and stone-ground crackers.

"Why don't we just say," Silver confessed, "that my dad was an
asshole!"

That got applause from the students with pierced body parts and tattoos of love and hate. He didn't need to explain.

"I'm glad to know you all," Silver crowed, bowing slightly. "Peace and love."

The audience clapped and rose to their feet, gathering their books and backpacks. Silver heard one female student ask, "Why can't he teach here?" He smiled at this compliment. He then smiled at the punk with candies.

"I hate my dad, too," the punk said as he tucked his skateboard under his arm. "I didn't know Hispanics had shitty fathers, too." He flung up an arm, and a candy twirled in the air.

Silver caught it with his left hand.

A box of Hot Tamales.

After the reading, Professor Wallace bought Silver a steak sandwich but didn't offer him a place to stay. Silver hinted only once. He hinted that he was sleepy, which was true, and that he couldn't drive at night, also true. The professor pretended not to hear.

Even with a steak sandwich in his hands, Silver fell into a funk because it meant that he would have to turn his car around and drive back without sleep. But his mood improved when the professor produced from the pocket inside his coat an envelope with the crispy sound of a cellophane window. For Silver, it meant only one thing: his four-hundred-dollar check.

"We appreciate your coming all this way," Professor Wallace said, then volunteered wistfully after he gazed around the restaurant, "You're lucky you don't have to teach."

Silver shook his hand, soft with chalk dust and the printed words of dead poets and writers, and watched the professor disappear, one shoulder more slumped than the other. Hunchbacked from carrying books, his body was sliding toward old age.

Silver drove out of Simi Valley, up the Tehachapi Ridge and into the San Joaquin Valley, which stunk of pesticides whirling in the wind. His windshield picked up a hundred gnats, bees, and yellow butterflies, a psychedelic experience in itself. Near Coalinga he grew exhausted, his eyelids heavy as magnets. He pulled onto the side of the freeway, some distance from the knifing flashes of oncoming cars and diesels. He slept sitting up, mouth agape, and toward dawn he woke with a stiff neck. He had parked next to what he assumed was a boulder, but when he rubbed his eyes, he saw a dead cow with its grassy hooves in the air.

"Shit." Silver whistled through his mustache. He had smelled something pitifully wrong all night but would never have surmised it was the cow he nearly hit earlier on the way down to Simi Valley.

He poked at the cow with his shoe. He pulled on the legs so that its death would be more modest, the testicles wagging out of view of the freeway traffic. No human or animal should be cast into death with its legs in the air. The cow rolled over with a long and final moan of air caught in its lungs.

Silver left the cow and drove back to Oakland, stopping once to treat himself at a Dairy Queen because he had sold three books.

On the steps of his duplex apartment, he was greeted by his housemate, Jamal Henry.

"Jamal," Silver called as he got out of the car.

Jamal's eyes were smoking.

"What's wrong, man?" Silver asked, walking stiffly from the car. His shoes were off.

"You got to go!" Jamal growled.

"What do you mean?" Silver asked, palms out. Silver stood on the first step of the porch. The toes of his socks were loose, his feet those of a jester during Shakespeare's time.

Jamal munched on his lower lip.

"It means that I got a new dude to live with. It means you're a lazy ass and I need a brother who can pay on the first. *Entiendes?*"

Silver rattled the check from Lowell College.

"I got paid," Silver claimed. "I can do it!"

"No, man, you got to go." Jamal crossed his arms across his chest. He stood like a sentry in front of the door.

From behind Jamal appeared a young Korean man.

"This here dude"—Jamal gestured—"he's got a scholarship and shit. Studying engineering for his country. I *know* he's going to pay." He turned to the young man. "Ain't that right?"

The Korean student nodded.

"But we go back, Jamal," Silver pleaded. They had more than once taken their poetry and music (Jamal on congas) to the streets. In their time together, they had gathered enough money and telephone numbers from women to validate their status in the creative world. Money always confirmed success.

"I'm sorry, but living in my pad is a business transaction and not like the Richmond Rescue Mission." Jamal cut a fiery glance at the porch, where Silver's clothes, stereo, CDs, and old records lay piled, plus a few cups, plates, and saucers. A mattress with sheets leaned against the window.

The door closed on Silver, and Silver, unsure what to do, sat on the steps of the porch. He peeled off his socks. He opened up the envelope and looked at the check. He saw that it was for $337.67.

"Damn!" he muttered.

The college had taken out money for federal and state taxes.

He gathered his stuff, including the mattress, and stuffed it in his Honda. He had been evicted several times from apartments and each time, he reasoned as he started the Honda, things worked out, although he did notice that with each departure, life got slightly harder for him. Still, he was hurt that Jamal, a buddy, would throw him out. Didn't they share a girlfriend once and plenty of street gigs?

He tried to cash the check, but because he didn't have enough money in his savings account, he had to walk out of the bank empty-handed.

"Damn again!" he growled. He climbed into his Honda and drove to his mother's place in Hayward, his eyes leering at the gas gauge. His mother wasn't home, so he climbed through her kitchen window, leaving a shoe print in the sink. He took a long shower, constructed himself a sandwich with three kinds of meats and cheeses, and slept on the couch with his knees tucked into his chest. He was startled awake a little after three when his mother whacked him with a coat hanger.

"What are you doing here?"

He woke sleepily. His mother was a blur behind the snotty cataracts of sleep. He rubbed his fists against his eyes.

"Sleeping," he answered truthfully.

His mother worked as the foreman in an industrial laundry off Freeway 880. She gave off the smell of soap and steam. It appeared that steam was rising from her hair.

"It's not time to sleep!" she snapped at him. "Night is when you sleep. Day is when you work." Her hands came up and propped themselves on her hips, padded with fat. "And I got a job for you, *menso!*"

Silver sat up at the word *job.*

"Where?"

His mother pointed to herself.

"With me!"

She suggested that he start his working career shoveling towels and sheets into the vat of boiling suds. The person who had been doing that task had burned his arms and face. He wasn't coming back until the bandages came off his eyes.

Silver stood up, wobbly, because he was still nearly asleep. He considered for a moment that maybe he was asleep and that what he was hearing was the start of a nightmare. He was not meant for lowly work. He needed his eyes to see where he was going.

"Nah, Mom, I can't work like that."

"And I can?" she asked, stabbing a stubby finger on her heart.

Steam rose from her hair. "I work in hell and you sleep like an angel in my house. No, sir!" She scrunched up her mouth, not unlike Jamal, except there was lipstick on her face. She added a twist of anger: "And who reads your poetry? Tell me that!"

Silver lowered his gaze to his toes, the bones nearly showing through his thin skin. She knew how to hurt a man.

"Huh, is that the idea?" she continued.

Silver had avoided work since he was twenty-one and was one of the grooviest fry cooks in Oakland. He worked for Hamburger Hut, and while he sweated over the hellish flames, he got to eat for free and occasionally pinched the buttocks of the waitresses, who gratefully quacked their pleasure. Only one time did a waitress strike him with a fry pan.

"Nah, Mom," he agreed. "That ain't the idea. The idea here is that I can't get no work."

"I said I can get you a job!" she bawled back.

"No, Mom, with my poetry."

She sneered.

He contemplated pulling the envelope from Lowell College and slapping her with the fact that he had just done a reading there, that he was in business, and that he had money in the bank waiting to clear. But his hand simply reached for his shirt pocket, scratched, and fell back to his side.

"Jamal threw me out," he informed her, batting his eyelashes. Surely she didn't wish her son to be reduced to pushing a Safeway cart from one end of Oakland to the other.

"And that's what I'm doing, too."

She stomped to the front door and threw it open. Sunlight knifed the carpet. Dust motes came alive and Poky, her dog with a snout like a shark, appeared and pressed his face into the screen door.

"It's for your own goddamn good!"

Silver slipped in his socks and shoes and left with a noose of shame around his skinny neck. He left humming a blues song about a lonely soul who laments that no one loves him but his mother and he ain't sure about her.

Now he was sure.

From a pay phone at a gas station, Silver called a few friends, but he only got answering machines with long stretches of salsa music before the voices sounded for the caller to leave a message. But he reached Enrique Rodriguez, a poet friend who was now a curator at a yuppito art gallery in San Francisco. Enrique changed his voice, pretending to be Enrique's housemate.

"I know it's you, Enrique!" Silver scolded.

"No, I'm Peter," said Enrique, his voice up on high heels. "Enrique is in Denver for an opening."

Silver hung up, gassed up his car with three dollars, and drove to Miguel Ramirez's place in Berkeley. Miguel, a successful photographer with plenty of money, lived in a loft with his dog, Humo.

Silver called from downstairs to windows tall as coffins.

"Miguel!" he yelled in the megaphone of his cupped hands. His words were whipped around by the wind from the bay, but he knew that some of them reached the window. "Miguel! It's me, man! You'll never guess what happened."

No one responded, though Silver could swear that he saw shadows flit across the window. At first he thought that it was Humo the dog, pacing the floor. Then he realized that no dog could walk on his hind legs and pour coffee into a cup and sip.

That night, Silver pulled his mattress onto a grassy strip outside Miguel's loft and slept under the godless stars.

Silver woke slowly, noise quivering rabbitlike, though his nostrils were hardly a cute bunny part. Through his closed eyes he imagined that he was sleeping next to the dead cow discovered on the side of the freeway outside of Coalinga. His nose momentarily stopped pulsating. A horrible stench enveloped his first waking moments, though he suspected his senses were all out of whack from allergies. He remembered parking his bones on newly mowed grass and under a pine tree with its bestiary of squirrels, robins, and torn kites. How could this be? He sniffed, coughed, and stretched until a bone clicked in his neck. In stretching, his hands felt what he supposed to be an udder and went so far as jerking it for a spot of milk. Alas, the udder turned out to be a finger.

"Shit!" he screamed. He jumped off the mattress and glared at the man with whom he had shared the comforts of a thin mattress. He knew himself to be a heavy sleeper, one who could snore through heavy metal or gangster rap. There was no telling what sordid things had happened to his body last night with this stranger, whose face looked to have been raked by a tumbleweed. He spanked his palms, hoping the friction of this action would scatter any germs. He made a mental note not to eat from his hands until they were washed.

The man shot his knees to his chest. He touched his stomach, opened a single yellow eye, and groaned not unlike the cow when the poor beast rolled over. The man rolled onto his side, lungs sacked with a snotty cold.

Silver moved away, considering himself lucky to be alive, apparently unscathed. He quickly examined his arms and body for wounds, and all seemed well. There was no telling whether this filthy person was recently exiled from a state hospital and dumped in Berkeley to trip around Telegraph Avenue with the other madmen.

Silver walked the hundred paces to Miguel's place, turning back twice to see for himself what kind of life he, a poet, was now leading.

"Miguel!" Silver meowed with his hands at his side. No way was he going to bring his paws to his face until they were washed.

A shadow cut across the window. The shadow had a telephone

in one hand and a coffee cup in the other. Business and pleasure, Silver surmised. It's got to be Miguel.

"Miguel!" Silver called desperately. He shot a nervous glance at the person on his mattress. On hands and knees, he appeared to be throwing up.

Miguel opened a window.

"Who goeth? Who calleth at my abode?" he asked in a fake English accent. "'Tis my love?"

"Me," Silver whimpered, though he considered momentarily answering, "Nah, it's yo momma!" But he was no mood to play, and furthermore, he wasn't certain if Manny cared a hoot for his mother, now a bitter word in Silver's own vocabulary. From his parched throat, Silver uttered his first complete sentence of the day: "It's fucked out here!"

When a buzzer sounded like an electric razor, Silver scrambled for the glass door, which he strained to push open, a workout in itself for the groovy set who lived in these stylish lofts. He raced to the third floor, taking great leaps up the stairwell.

The door to Miguel's loft was open. Silver was greeted by Humo, an Irish setter who dutifully back-stepped, allowing him the space to enter.

Natural light poured coolly through the large, industrial-sized windows. The smell of coffee circled the air. Silver had heard that Miguel had uncovered the riches of commercial photography, but he never imagined that Miguel could afford this clean and well-ordered space in a trendy building filled with people with yuppito attitudes. Everyone else he knew in the arts had housemates who hoarded canned food under their beds. Silver sized up the surroundings like a hick in New York City. He was impressed by the uncluttered effect of Miguel's contemporary furniture and the artsy-smartsy, slick magazines on a coffee table—the thinner the magazine, the more costly. Framed photographs were mounted on the walls. Yellow fish with red lips swam in an aquarium that hummed on a bookshelf. Silver was impressed by the high ceiling and the wall-mounted Bang & Olufsen, whose speakers bleated Celtic music.

"Cool place," he remarked.

Although he was a poet, he had not words for the steel sink in the kitchen; it was long enough for a cadaver to be examined. Instead of a cadaver, however, there was a plate of bagels and a single puny coffeepot that emitted steam and the savory aroma of French roast.

During his Chicano activist days in the midseventies, in which he was beaten by cops from San Diego to Redding, Miguel realized one day that he should get on with a career. This decision came moments after a cop clubbed the middle of his forehead, raising a horn of tissue that didn't go down for a month. During that month his female friends began to call him "horny" when he turned this appendage into an erotic asset that no other man could boast of. More than one girlfriend called the horn on his face more exciting than the one between his legs.

Miguel's trade was now his photography, and he did everything from fashion shoots to computer graphics. He also worked with a private investigator, a used-up professional football player named J. J. Albert. J. J. hired him to videotape the aftermath of car wrecks, industrial accidents, and scenes of crimes. The last shoot involved a broker who threw his client twenty stories to a screaming death. Miguel videotaped the asphalt, undented by the impact; something about proving the death was painful.

Though less glamorous, these jobs brought him gobs of easy money because insurance companies were involved.

"You look like shit," Miguel remarked as he came out of the bathroom. The remark echoed off the walls so that Silver had to hear it three times. Miguel made his way into the kitchen and poured Silver a cup of coffee.

"Can I use your head?" Silver asked.

"Don't talk nasty," Miguel joked.

"I'm all dirty."

Miguel threw Silver a dish towel and warned him not to use the towels in the bathroom. Silver was too desperate to feel insulted. He took the towel and scrubbed his face and neck until his skin was pink as the underside of a starfish. He rinsed his mouth and sprinkled water on his hair. Forgoing the silver-plated brush set on the counter, he used his fingers to comb his oily locks into a semblance of order. His razor was in the car, as was his toothbrush. But he rifled through a drawer, brought out the toothpaste, and brushed his teeth with two fingers. He exhaled a minty fire, spotting the mirror with his breath.

He intended to keep a low profile while staying with Miguel. That is, if Miguel agreed to let him sleep on the couch for a day or two. He scolded the reflection in the mirror, "You better behave! *Entiendes?*"

Silver returned to the living room for his coffee. He sipped and wiped his mustache, careful not to let a single drop of morning brew cascade to the floor.

"So what you been up to?" Miguel asked with his eyes on the screen of his computer monitor. His eyes were sparking green from the glowing words. He was checking his E-mail.

Silver considered hovering over Miguel's shoulder, but he remembered the promise he had made to himself in the bathroom. He kept his distance, sitting on the couch, his legs together and his hands on his lap. He didn't want to spread himself around Miguel's space.

"I was just down in L.A., giving a poetry reading," Silver remarked after his first sip of coffee. The brew kicked in his stomach. Silver could already feel his bowels loosen; a second trip to the bathroom was imminent. Still, he yammered about the dead cow on the side of the freeway and the punk kid with his arm caught in the vending machine. He giggled, encouraging Miguel to laugh along at his misadventure. He described three times the Baby Ruth candy bars flying in the air and the students snatching them like frogs catching flies.

Miguel forced a smile, unmoved.

"And now I got this problem," Silver said.

Miguel looked up, appraised Silver, who had brought his hands back to his lap, and returned his gaze to the computer screen. He sensed a request was forthcoming.

"We're having our house fumigated," Silver lied. He spread his index finger from his thumb to show how large cockroaches had gotten in east Oakland. "I need a place to stay for two nights, three at the most. Jamal's at his mother's, and my mom . . . ," he said, but he couldn't lie on this point: "She hates me because I won't get a regular job."

If Miguel had feigned interest, it stopped when the computer began to spit out a fax. He licked his lips, wrote down an address on a yellow pad, and closed down the computer.

"I got a job," he announced. He stood up, hands massaging the small of his back, and picked up the signal that Silver was hungering for the bagels in the kitchen. "Go ahead. Chow down."

While Miguel searched a map of the East Bay, Silver sliced open a bagel and smacked it with loads of cream cheese. He ate and sipped his coffee, then used the rest room, flushing twice from the frightening mess he created in the bowl. When he came out, Miguel said, "Let's go, man."

"You're the boss," Silver replied.

Silver didn't care where they were going as long as he could shadow Miguel, who, he assessed from the fact that he was set up for E-mail, was a success, one of the few from the Chicano *movimiento* who had made it. Even a *Money* magazine sat on the coffee table.

Miguel shrugged into a safari-type jacket. They made their way to the garage and got into Miguel's Volkswagen Bug, newly designed and still with the new-car smell. They left via a gate that opened electronically.

"Now, this is a nice car," Silver crowed. "Just like the old ones, but nicer."

They sped smoothly around the corner of the building. Immediately the stranger on the mattress came into view. He was sitting up, shirtless, his legs folded in a yoga position. He had the pinched waist of a red ant.

"Bums are sleeping all over the place," Miguel remarked. His voice was neither vicious nor compassionate. It was a matter-of-fact comment. It was the truth.

Silver swallowed.

"Yeah, I've noticed," he said in a near whisper. "The world is changing."

They banked the corner, and Silver swiveled his eyes toward his Honda, parked at a meter. A parking ticket was clipped behind the windshield wiper. One more, Silver realized, and his ride risked a tow to the graveyard of unclaimed cars. He averted his eyes from the sorry soul on the mattress.

Miguel explained a second time that he was often hired to videotape accidents and such, and these images, unbiased footage, were used by the defense or prosecution. Either way, it didn't matter to him.

"That's weird," Silver said. He never knew such a business as Miguel's existed. It sounded easy.

They drove to a chained lot with crushed cars. A black man in overalls sat under an umbrella, his heavy hands like wrenches on his thick, Santa Claus lap. A silent radio was at his feet.

Miguel cut the engine and popped the hood of the trunk, situated up front like in the old Bugs. He studied the computer spreadsheet of his assignment from J. J. Albert. "It's the motor they're asking for." For Silver, Miguel glossed over the report of a business type in a suit and tie and how he had gotten out of the car when it began to overheat. He opened the hood and peered in. The fan belt sucked him right in.

"Poor dude," said Silver as he boosted himself out of the car. He grimaced. He saw red meat thin as credit cards. "That's a terrible way to go, all sliced up."

"Nah, he just broke his neck," Manny argued, twisting his own neck until it popped with tension. "He didn't feel a thing. His three children are going to feel it."

Without bothering to get up, the guard gave a mock salute, allowing Miguel and Silver to pass. They walked among the wrecked cars until they came to a 1998 Audi, nearly new and sparkling like knives under a soft coat of dust.

Miguel read the computer printout, then the license plate. This was their baby, he pointed out. With the hood already cracked, Miguel asked Silver to open the latch.

Silver stepped back, scared. He imagined that under the hood were body parts—an eyeball on top of the manifold, a pair of bloody lips near the clutch, a finger sitting on some doodad. Hair was probably flung all over like in a barbershop.

"Don't tell me you're scared," Miguel taunted. "I thought poets worked with death."

"Yeah, but only on the page." But Silver realized that wasn't true either because most of his poems were about protesting Chicanos. He placed in the back of his mind the notion that perhaps it was time he wrote about death, seeing that his face was pleated with wrinkles and wiry gray hairs were camping in his mustache.

When Miguel raised the hood, Silver squealed, "Ahhh," his hands flying to his face to fend off the gruesome scene.

But the engine was clean. Miguel unshouldered his video camera, brought the cap off the lens, and began recording from overhead on tiptoes, leaning his body against the grille. The job was done before Silver could unwrinkle the grimace on his face.

Silver peered into the engine, not unlike a casket, and gazed around its compact compartment. A chill pinched his shoulders. He pictured a man sucked into the fan and sliced to death on the shoulder of the freeway.

Silver raised his hand to his throat and applied a gentle pressure. "Shit," he gurgled when he increased the pressure. He imagined a horrible and ignominious death. He warned himself never to sport a tie while the hood of his Honda was up.

Back in the car, Silver was silenced by Miguel's attention on his cell phone. He eavesdropped on Miguel's private business, something about a photo shoot at the Golden Gate Bridge on Thursday. He listened to him talk about an overdue bill with his accountant and then coo to a woman about their evening ahead. They were going to meet at an art opening.

While Miguel punched yet another number, this one purely business because his face was flat, Silver turned his attention to the scene out the window. He marveled for the first time at a bright shopping center. A tide of cars was pulling away and another tide was pulling in, a commercial flux that would make any businessman happy. Silver wished he could join the shoppers, be one of the crowd. He imagined his hand reaching for his wallet to buy something frivolous, a single rose or an ice cream cone. He was tired of his years of drifting. He aimed to change his life since his kind—those devoted to the Chicano *movimiento*—were disappearing. He had lost thirteen pounds to prove that he was disappearing.

After Miguel got off the phone with a client in Millbrae, Silver waited a respectful two minutes before he inquired, subtly he thought, about a career change.

"So, how do you work a video thing like you got?"

Silver received the okay from Miguel to stay two nights. But if Miguel should bring home a female friend, then Silver had to go. Miguel waved a hand in the air, indicating that his loft was huge but finally only one room and without privacy. He couldn't have Silver on the couch eating an apple or a banana while he and his date were getting it on.

"I can't let you in on my love techniques," he said with a straight face, then burst out laughing.

Silver nodded. He hoped Miguel's date was a dog.

"So how long you got to stay out of your place?" Miguel asked.

Silver, head tilted, offered a puzzled look.

"The fumigation," Miguel reminded him.

Silver's eyed widened. "Oh, that," he started. "Just like what you said I could stay here—two days."

Crowding in for the truth, Miguel asked, "You're lying, huh?"

"Nah, I ain't lying," Silver, a bad actor, lied. He held up two fingers in the V shape of victory. "Two days and I'm outta here and back where I belong."

Miguel lowered his eyes to the floor, then directed them to Humo, whose tail was brushing against the cement floor.

"Do me a favor and walk the dog." He had work to catch up on.

At the word *walk*, Humo fetched his leash and brought it to Miguel, who hooked the leash onto the collar. He handed the lead to Silver.

Silver was pulled down the stairwell and out the front door. At the first tree, protected by a wire cage, Humo raised a leg skirted with a fringe of orange fur and squirted a powerful shot that could have stopped a skunk. The dog sniffed his accomplishment and pulled Silver up the street.

"Go easy, dude!" Silver demanded.

Humo led him across the street in the direction of Silver's temporary sleeping quarters—the mattress and the man with whom—he couldn't believe it—he had spent a night. To Silver, it seemed like fate that a dog should haul him to where he had bottomed out in life, or what he hoped was the bottom. He contemplated yanking on Humo's leash but recalled the gagging sensation when he squeezed his own throat to evaluate his threshold for pain. He followed the pull of Humo's will to join a puppy, seemingly lifeless, in the arms of the person on the mattress.

Silver greeted the stranger with a "hey."

The man was shivering. His cavernous eyes were watering, and he appeared more whipped than the pup in his lap.

"Does your dog bite?" the man asked. He cuddled the pup protectively. "Master isn't feeling too good."

"Nah, he's cool." Silver gauged the pup's condition and then looked over at his Honda. The windshield wiper gripped yet another ticket.

Humo licked the pup, but the pup was too weak to lick back with the same ferocity. He simply let his tongue poke out, roll, and return to the cage of his furry mouth.

Humo caught sight of a bird and pulled Silver in its direction, but not before Silver picked up the pleading sounds of the man moaning, "My stomach hurts."

"I think you need something to eat," Silver suggested.

The man blinked.

Silver retrieved fresh underwear and his toothbrush and shaver out of his car. With Humo at his side, he made his way to the Taco Bell at the corner and bought two bean-and-meat burritos. He took them to the stranger, though he hoped that the sickly puppy might take a nibble as well.

"These might hit the spot." Silver turned quickly before he became even more involved with this person. He wanted to show charity, nothing more.

But the man called, "My name's Roberto. What's yours?"

Silver couldn't pretend not to hear. With Humo pulling on the leash, he wheeled his head around and answered, "Silver." Right then, he realized this exchange of first names was a mistake. Why chum up with a street person?

Late that afternoon, Silver and Miguel showered and got ready for a photography opening in San Francisco. Miguel lent Silver some clothes. The sports jacket, while out of style and loose on his skinny frame, improved Silver's confidence. He paraded in front of the mirror and then out the door when Miguel called, "Let's go, homes! The *rucas* are waiting."

"So who's exhibiting?" Silver asked.

The traffic was slow on the freeway, but at least they were moving.

"Ralph," Miguel answered after a long silence. His eyes were fixed on the rearview mirror and on the tailgater behind him.

Silver thought for a moment. "Ralph who?"

"They just call him Ralph."

Silver's confidence didn't lose its starch even when he entered the gallery that was all glass and track lighting and immediately came upon Enrique, his poet friend turned yuppito curator, the one who was supposed to be at another opening. He wasn't sure where, but then recalled Denver.

"Asshole," Silver whispered.

"What?" Miguel asked.

"Nothing," Silver said, then chirped, "Nice space."

Miguel shoved off toward a woman with red hair. Her eyebrows were tortured with pins. The redhead smiled widely at Miguel; a ball bearing was attached to her tongue.

"Jesus!" Silver swore. He liked his women with regular tongues and without hardware hanging from their eyebrows. He remembered when it was radical to get a single earring. Now the young kids were pincushions.

Silver meandered through the gallery, sizing up the crowd, and eventually confronted the photographs, all black and whites of—*híjole!* he could have screamed—male genitals of less than spectacular dimensions. Was this Chicano art? Was the new hype not to have a last name? He presumed only dogs and cats didn't have last names.

Enrique beamed brightly at Silver, zigzagged through the crowd, and cried, "Silver!"

Silver couldn't help it. "Eat shit, Ernie!"

Enrique's hand went to his mouth. He was smiling behind his hand. "Oh, my. You haven't grown up."

Silver slapped Ernie's hand away and went his own way. He appraised the crowd, now young and seemingly affluent, all with knobs, pins, and gizmos stabbed on their faces. He considered his outburst at Enrique. Perhaps he hadn't grown up and it was time that he did. But it was too late for that fucker. He eyed the hors d'oeuvres—the sight of shrimp forced his nostrils to flare—and pushed his way between a girl couple to get a plate, which was ceramic, not paper, a sign that the food was above the usual fodder of art openings. He loaded his plate but not so high that he had to watch it at all moments.

He ate his goodies while facing the photograph of a male's uncircumcised organ. People collect this crap? he wondered. They live with it on their walls? He bit into a garlic shrimp, chewed until his mouth was clean, and snarled, "This is *pura caca!*"

"You don't like the shrimp?" a young woman asked. She had been standing over his shoulder, towering, in fact, on platforms that were close to stilts.

Silver turned his head as he wiped his mouth. "No, it's tasty." He looked down at his plate. "Even the zucchini is good stuff. I was talking about the photos."

She lifted her eyebrows. She wanted to know what was *pura caca* about them, but she couldn't coax from Silver his private thoughts regarding the photographs. So she asked, "Are you a teacher?"

Silver shook his head.

"You look like a teacher."

"Nah, baby, I'm not. I taught once, but the paycheck never showed up. Took three months to get paid."

She smiled.

Silver prayed that she would go away, but he remembered Enrique's remark about not growing up. So it was time to chitchat: "Nah, I'm a poet. Silver Mendez. I got a couple of books out." He proceeded to rake the shrimp on his plate over a puddle of peanut sauce.

The excited woman stomped her foot and then touched Silver's sleeve. "You're kidding. You're not Silver Mendez! The poet?"

Silver felt flattered. He pinched at his mustache, searching for crumbs embedded in its bristles. He held back a lavish smile until he rolled his tongue over the front of his teeth.

"Oh, wow," the young woman crowed. "My grandma used to read your work."

Silver's smile flattened.

But the young woman's smile widened. A ball bearing was attached to her tongue, too. Her mouth closed along with her eyes. She clicked her fingers and, searching her memory, asked, "What's that poem, something about oranges and how you went out on your first date and didn't have any money?"

"That describes me how I am now. I don't have any money now," he said. He laughed, but not much.

"Get outta here!" She sipped from her wine and scanned the crowd with her nose in her drink and her eyes wheeling about. To Silver, she resembled an alligator.

"You know," she said, smacking her lips, "the next guy I date is going to be an artist. Someone who works with blowtorches. I saw something about that on television. The guy had a really good tan."

Silver squeezed his eyes closed and walked away sightless, all the shrimp on his plate gone and the conversation with this woman just about done. When he bumped into another woman, he opened his eyes, offered a sincere, "Excuse me, I'm really sorry," and went to feign admiration for another pair of genitals, these far larger and sticky looking from some exodus of lovemaking, figured Silver.

Silver placed his empty plate on a table, wiped his mouth, and grabbed a white wine from a waiter gliding past. He gulped it in three noisy slurps and grabbed another one. While his personality was not tied to alcohol, he knew there were some moments when its effects were warranted. He faced such a moment now.

Instead of the photography, Silver looked out the window at a poor soul on the corner. He had an arm in a garbage can and was fishing for . . . a black sneaker, which he turned over and tossed in the gutter. The arm went back, stirring the can for its stinky valuables.

"Poor dude," Silver muttered.

Silver realized an alarmingly short distance separated him from that lowly person, just a thickness of plate glass and the clean clothes—all borrowed from Miguel, socks included—on his body. He downed the second glass of wine. He had to keep that distance, even if it meant smooching Enrique's face. Smooch, smooch. Perhaps he had to grow up and learn a new way to conduct his life. While he had a name in the seventies, his value had fallen off; now if he reached into his pocket—Miguel's pocket— he fingered lint. He needed a job, something like Miguel's, where there was both money and adventure. The last thing he wanted was to move dirty towels and sheets into a vat of hot soapy water. Anyone could do that. Even him.

Miguel got the date he was patrolling for, and Silver, kicking a pebble on the sidewalk, was plainly out of luck.

"Like I told you," Miguel said, squeezing Silver's arm as the two stood in front of Miguel's loft in Berkeley. "If something came my way, *pues*, I was going to act." He broke the news while the two stood in the dark, and above in the loft Humo peered down on the scene, whimpering.

"Yeah, like you said," Silver agreed, trying to lighten the moment. "You don't want to let your love secrets out."

Miguel patted Silver's arm.

Silver started to leave, but Miguel called him back.

"I need my coat," Miguel said directly.

"I thought the jacket was out of style."

"Yeah, but it's coming back. That's what someone told me."

Silver slipped it off and would have taken off the shirt and pants angrily, but Miguel's date had just rounded the corner in a tiny SUV. He and Miguel were caught in her headlights. Why make a scene?

Miguel's date got out of her car, and her legs were long, spiderlike. The legs, Silver saw, belonged to the woman who confused him with the poet who wrote a romantic poem about oranges and whose next date was going to be an artist who worked with a blowtorch. Silver shielded his face as he started to hurry away, though he heard her say, "I'll tell my grandma I saw you."

Silver returned to his Honda, pumped the gas pedal, and tried to turn over the engine. But the battery was down.

"Shit," he scolded the steering wheel.

He turned on the headlights and their dull, yellowish beam glowed on the person on the mattress. He resembled a lost sailor on a raft, thin as rope and with a face full of whiskers. His lips were red from smacking for something hardy to eat. Silver quickly cut off the headlights, banging his fist against the steering wheel. He hung his head and knew what was coming when footsteps crunched over leaves and gravel. He uncurled his hands and gazed at the lines on his palms that revealed a long life. But why a long life with poor people? he asked himself. Why couldn't he live in a loft like Miguel's?

He felt his Honda rock.

"Hey, Silver," Roberto called with his hands on the doorjamb. "It's me, Roberto. Roll down your window."

93

Two hours ago he was with the fast Hispanic set and now he was peering into the watery eyes of the future. The future looked murky.

"I'm sleeping! Can't you see!" Silver screamed through the rolled-up window. His breath fogged the glass with his scolding tirade. He felt ashamed because he usually only mouthed off to people in power, and this living nightmare outside his car had barely enough power to lower and raise his zipper. Silver saw that his zipper was undone. Perhaps he lacked the power for even that small effort.

"You look like you're awake to me."

The window cleared of his angry breath after a moment of silence. Silver's anger receded as well. "I got to get some shut-eye," Silver informed Roberto.

Roberto cast a glance at Miguel's loft. He pointed. "I thought you lived there."

Salt on a tender wound.

Silver rolled down the window. He studied the man, whose face was splotched red and whose shoulder-length hair was tangled. "Nah, man, I don't live there."

"Where do you live, then?" Roberto asked.

More salt for his wounds.

But Silver answered truthfully. "Looks like I live in my car. You wanna get in?"

Roberto slid into the car, and his odor was deadlier than secondhand smoke.

"Man, you got a smell about you."

Roberto looked hurt.

"Come on, dude," Silver said. "Let's wash up."

The two got out of the car. Silver doused Roberto's hands with water from a plastic jug, and Roberto wrung them until the grime gave way to pink skin. Silver fetched a bar of soap from the glove compartment for a second washing. Then Silver asked Roberto to strip off his pants and shirt, plus his underwear, which had Silver wincing at the holocaust that dwelt in its cotton. Silver searched in his plastic bag for a new set of clothes—white pants and an orange sweater. Under the streetlight and a moon wrecked with dents and useless myths, Roberto became a changed man. He shook Silver's hand and called him "my buddy."

Silver accepted the thanks but had doubts about them being buds.

The two got back into the Honda.

"I feel better." Roberto sighed, a swimmer coming up from a dive in cold water.

"You got to work on your breath." Silver put a finger to his lip and thought. "Nah, I thought I had another toothbrush. It's a comb I'm thinking of."

"God, I feel better," Roberto repeated. "I promise when I talk, I'll turn my head."

The two sat in silence, then talked about the most unusual places they had slept. For Silver it was in a tree outside a girl's window, resulting in near strangulation when her real boyfriend, a wrestler with a canned ham for a heart, showed up. For Roberto, it was the county jail in Livermore.

"That don't sound weird," Silver said.

"It is if you're around dudes who want to turn you over and make you into a girl. In places like that, you got to stay awake."

"You don't have to worry about that tonight, homes," Silver said. "I like girls and like beds, too, except I'm out of luck on both fronts."

They grew groggy and finally fell asleep, side by side, until in the gray smudgings of dawn they heard a humming vehicle that honked none too politely, its beady-eyed headlights glaring in the Honda's rearview mirror.

"What the hell!" Silver cursed. He winced and looked over his shoulder at a monster of a machine. For a hazy moment, he imagined that he was in a scene of a low-budget space movie, something about an alien machine eating up Mexicans.

"Hey, you gonna move, man?" the driver of the street sweeper screamed over the idling engine.

Silver rolled down the window. "Battery's dead. Gimme a push."

"Nah, I ain't giving you a push," the driver said. "You gonna sue me if I fuck up yo' car."

Silver promised that he wouldn't sue him or anyone else. He told the city worker that every Chicano lawyer he knew, he owed money to. Who would defend him?

"I just trying to do my job," the worker cried like the blues. "And now I gotta be like Triple A."

The street sweeper driver fumed but finally edged his monster machine against the Honda's back fender. The Honda jerked and rolled until it reached the speed a dime takes when it falls from a hand and hurries away. Silver popped the clutch and the Honda kicked alive, a fist of black smoke dissolving in the air.

Silver waved to the street sweeper, who ignored his thanks and got to work clearing more garbage from the streets of Berkeley.

Silver pointed the car south on 880.

"I haven't been in a car in almost a year," said Roberto, smiling at the skyline of San Francisco across the bay. "It's nice." He asked Silver where they were headed.

"Hayward," he answered. "They got jobs over there."

Although the traffic was heavy with morning commuters, they arrived at Ace Laundry at six-thirty, in time to lean against the factory building and wait for Silver's mother. Silver bragged about his mother, who he claimed had pull with the owner, a race-horse owner. The owner paid everyone poorly so he could do what he really wanted to do: lose money at the track. Or so Silver heard from his mother.

The Ace Laundry building was brick and resembled a penitentiary Al Capone called home in the 1930s. With a fingernail,

Silver scratched his name on the face of a brick. This would be his testimony of labor, other than the labor he knew when he licked a pencil and wrote poetry. He scrawled *"pinche cabrón"* on a second brick, then decided this was too childish and erased it with spit. With time to kill, Silver told Roberto that he was a poet.

"What does a poet do?" Roberto asked innocently.

The question cut like a razor. Looking back on his career of two books and too many nearly lassoed literary prizes that offered no money but a mild token of prestige, he wasn't sure what he had accomplished. As to other Chicano poets, he wasn't confident that their accomplishments amounted to a hill of beans, either. Still, he tried to offer a description. He said a poet was a man or woman who wrote human thoughts in a beautiful and true order in a lunatic world. That's what first came to mind. A poet was a person who suffered, though there was some consolation in drink and momentary screwing with people you already knew. He looked at the brick in the factory wall. A poet was someone who attempted to become immortal, even if the poet had to make scratches on bricks that a hard rain would wash away.

"A poet," Silver added, "is a dude like you or me. You know, it's about how you talk. . . ."

Roberto nodded, lost.

"Talk is like poetry. Just get the shit going."

When Silver's mother arrived, walking down the path from the parking lot, he was surprised to see her arm around a small Filipino man. Next to her, the man was small as a child, his smile like a spoon drawer from all the silver in his teeth. It never occurred to Silver that his mother could be messing around at her age, sixty-one, he guessed from tallying his own years on the planet, but he had eyes in his head and could see for himself.

"Mom!" he called.

His mother pulled her arm off the man's shoulders. She

stopped in her boot-printed tracks, and the man glided past into the door of the factory.

"What are you doing here?" she asked.

She gave off the scent of perfume, which surprised Silver because he had the notion that washed hands and a face was all that was required to work in a factory. He didn't know that you had the option to smell good at the beginning of your shift.

"Who's the dude?" he asked.

"None of your business." Again she asked what he was doing here. If he was here to ask for money, then he could take a hike. She made a hitchhiking sign for emphasis.

"Me and my friend Roberto, we're looking for work." He explained that the two had met a few days ago but didn't mention they had shared a mattress on the ground or the compact sleeping quarters of his Honda. "I'm ready for work, like you said."

His mother grew angry. She had yet go into the factory, and already her head was steaming. One curl on her dyed head was unraveling.

"Roberto needs a job, and I need one, too." He pleaded with his mother by shivering and saying that he was cold and what better place to get warm but a factory with industrial washers and clouds of steam to clean him and his friend by lunchtime. He said that he would do anything, even the job of the guy who went blind. "Plus Roberto has this dog that's sick."

Roberto touched Silver's arm. "He's dead."

Silver jumped. "Dead? Master's dead?"

Roberto said that the pup had died last night and that he buried him in the flower bed in front of Miguel's loft.

Silver didn't want to know any more. And his mother didn't want to know any more, either. She guided them into an office where they signed papers that neither of them read.

"Get these smocks on," his mother, now Mrs. Mendez the foreman, commanded. She tossed the smocks in their faces.

Silver put the apron over his head.

"How do you this, Mom?" Silver asked, holding up the strings of the apron.

"It's not 'mom' here," she reminded him. "You didn't listen to me when you were a boy, but you're going to listen to me now." Her grip was like wrenches when she pulled on the strings and tied.

"I can hardly breathe." Silver laughed. He eyed his waist. "Looks like a girl's figure the way it's tied."

Within minutes they were pushing bins of hotel towels and sheets from the dock to machines that were noisy as the street sweeper. By close to eight the two were soaked from sweat and steam.

"I feel like a crab in hot water," Roberto said.

Silver struggled with an armful of towels, staggering toward a large washing machine. "I'm more than just hot."

Roberto's face wrinkled up, confused. "What's more than hot?"

"Bored."

Roberto nodded, shining with intelligence. "That's how come you're a poet, huh?"

"What do you mean?"

"You got two things happening at the same time—hot and bored. Usually I just think of one thing at a time."

They rolled the bins back for another load, this time sheets, and Silver smacked his lips and remarked that he would do anything for a beer.

"That's weird," Roberto said, pausing to catch his breath. "I was thinking the same thing. We're almost alike!"

Ten minutes before lunch, Silver and Roberto, faces and hands stained red, were prodded by his mother and her boss to the door. The boss booted open the door and yelled, "You're lucky that's not your ass!" They were tossed out with no more ceremony than two cardboard boxes heaved for the recycler.

Silver turned and hollered back, "Roberto didn't know!"

Roberto went beyond the duty of simply heaving a load of white rugs into the open vat and also tossed in three handfuls of soap. The soap, fragrant and loose as sand, was white crystals from an unmarked plastic bucket. But when the crystals hit the surface they exploded into red dye. Roberto, climbing down from a ladder that hung from the vat, didn't notice the chemical reaction. But Silver, climbing a ladder on the opposite side of the vat, did notice. His heart leaped under his wet smock. He imagined that Roberto had fallen in and was being cooked in the broth of his own anemic blood.

With less than eight hours of work between them, they were let go and threatened with police action.

"Mi'jo, you're so stupid!" his mother scolded.

He sneered at his mother the foreman. He again recalled the blues song about no one loving you but your mother and, hell, she was probably off the list, too. Now he knew for certain it applied to him. She wasn't going to get a Christmas present from him ever again.

His mother and boss disappeared into the factory, leaving Silver and Roberto like wet chickens, their hair pulled every which way. Red dye dripped from the ends of their noses.

"Shit," Silver muttered, then sneezed. He rubbed at his face, but the dye held.

"And I was just starting to like the job, too," Roberto wailed. He pouted and crossed his arms on his chest.

The two drove in silence toward Oakland, though for a brief moment Silver considered going to his mother's house and stealing the grub in her refrigerator, an act of vengeance that would certainly hurt because she loved to eat and read the newspaper in the solemn silence of her home. But this idea passed quickly because Silver wasn't keen on going to jail over bologna and canned ham. Instead he drove to his bank, his eyes falling toward the gas gauge needling toward empty. His check from Lowell College must have cleared by now, he thought.

"You keep your money here?" Roberto asked as the Honda bumped and rolled into the parking lot of the Walnut Bank. He asked this with his head ducked down and his eyes swiveling in their sockets. His breath was sour with fear.

"Yeah, why?" asked Silver. He cut the engine and fixed his eyes on the rearview mirror. He was surprised how a handful of crystals could change a person's appearance.

"I used to work here."

"Aw, bullshit," Silver retorted.

Roberto recounted how he used to work as a security guard at the Walnut Bank but quit a few years back when he could do better. He said that he didn't want Gus Hernandez, the remaining security guard, to see him in his current state of decomposition. Old Gus had warned him that life was hard outside the confines of one's abilities, which, for Roberto, was to open and close doors for customers in addition to preventing street people such as himself from drinking the free coffee. He never had to pull a gun on a robber, though he had to break up a fight between two brothers over a dollar-fifty. In the fracas, he got punched in the eye and got two days off to do nothing but watch television with his good eye.

"No shit!" Silver said. "You used to work here? As a guard!"

"Not so loud," Roberto begged.

Silver got out of the car and with his head in the window demanded loudly, "Tell me more about it later, okay? I'm going to get my money."

In the lobby of the bank Silver helped himself to a cup of coffee, which he laced with three packets of sugar. His stomach growled for a glazed doughnut, but there were none. He knew that with the dye on his mug he looked like an oddball. The incident at the factory was all an honest mistake, he told himself.

He and Roberto had tried to rescue the rugs, but they only splashed themselves like ducks with the tainted water. He reflected on this mishap as he sipped a second cup of coffee. His stomach again growled. He pushed the heel of his palm into his stomach until it shut up.

He sipped his hot brew, disregarding the security guard eyeing him openly. With coffee cup in hand, he got in line but froze: the woman he met at the photography show was one of the tellers. The line disappeared quickly.

"Damn," Silver muttered. He had heard that what goes around comes around, but this woman seemed to come into his life every few hours. He bristled over her confusion that he was the famous Chicano poet, all hot shit because he had a university job and wrote poems people liked. What did he know about pain?

"Hey!" the teller squealed playfully. "Did you like the opening? The shrimp was wow."

"Yeah, I guess," he answered flatly. "And you were at Miguel's."

Her loop earrings banged when she nodded, a twinkle in her devilish eye. She bit her lower lip like a little girl. But she was anything but a little girl: her legs were long and hurtful as scissors.

Silver noticed that she had bags under her eyes, the typical flaw of good-looking single women. But she looked happy as a bride. She had been a bride with a lot of guys, a newlywed over and over. Or so Silver surmised.

"I got to make this quick," Silver said anxiously. He asked for all his savings as he filled out a withdrawal slip.

But the teller couldn't help herself. "What's that on your face . . . and hands?"

"Ah, dye. It was an accident."

She remarked that red dye is used to mark stolen money. She described to Silver how she was almost robbed once, but the man changed his mind—he broke down crying and explained that he was dying of cancer and only wanted to live. She giggled and asked, "You ain't a bank robber, are you?"

"No, I'm an honest dude," Silver answered, and glanced over at the security guard, who was still keeping an eye on him. "Now if I can just get my money."

He withdrew every cent except a dollar, which she explained he needed to keep his account open.

"Nice seeing you." She stomped her feet and crooned, "I just love your poem 'Oranges.' It's so romantic."

Silver smiled but didn't bother to set her right about the authorship of the poem. He gave her a quick salute and was out the front door, a brisk wind thrust into his face that for a second made for difficult breathing. He got in the car, patting his front pocket and telling Roberto, "It's all here, homes."

When he tried to turn it over, the engine moaned.

"*Pinche cabrón!*" Silver yelled.

"I thought Hondas were supposed to be good." Roberto had resurfaced from the floor.

"Yeah, but of course not this one. That's because I own it."

The two got out of the car. With the help of Gus the security guard, who didn't recognize Roberto with all the dye on his face, they pushed the Honda until it sputtered alive.

"God, Gus got old," Roberto lamented as he looked through the back at the security guard, who was slapping his hands clean.

"It's the stupid alternator!" Silver said, exhausted and with sweat shiny as cellophane on his neck. "Who's Gus?"

"The guy I worked with. He's a really nice person." Roberto described how he had taught Gus English in the evenings and how in return Gus would make him killer potato-and-egg burritos.

But Silver faded out of the conversation. His mind was on the Honda, which he coaxed back to life when it stalled at a red light. He didn't see how knowing another Mexican would help him solve his current problem. He already knew more Mexicans than he wanted.

"Not again," he screamed at the car when it sputtered at the second red light.

This was Silver's luck. Once he got more than a hundred dollars in his pocket, the next thing he knew the car was begging for it. His cars were like junkies, ready for a fix.

They drove to a gas station in downtown Berkeley. With the car idling, Silver pumped five dollars' worth and then asked the mechanic, Hiro, how much it would cost to replace the alternator. He had to ask three times, since Hiro's hearing was gone and his guard dog was barking for a taste of Silver's legs. Hiro raised a pinkie to his face and blotted a tear from his eye, damaged from an accident.

"Your tires?" Hiro asked, peeking at the worn front set of tires.

"No, man, the alternator!" Silver screamed. "How much!"

Hiro shuffled to his office. He licked a thumb and opened a book huge as a telephone directory. With his glasses off and his face lowered over the pages, he worked slowly, his oil-stained index finger going down the columns as he muttered, "'Seventy-eight, 'seventy-nine, 'eighty, 'eighty-one." All this while Silver's car idled, sucking precious gas.

"Hundred and sixty," Hiro said calmly.

"No way!" Silver cried.

"That's for the part," Hiro added. "It's also . . . about a hundred dollars for labor."

"Aw, come on, man," Silver moaned. "That book's got to be wrong. This ain't a dealership!"

Hiro blinked, unmoved.

"Hell, I can drive down to Fresno, buy a whole new car at a chop shop for that price."

Hiro closed the book, pulled a tear from his tearing eye, and shuffled away with the attitude that you either had the money or didn't. The owner was looking for a customer who did.

Silver got in his car and slammed the door.

"So what did he say?" Roberto asked.

Silver sighed and sniffed the air.

"Now is the car on fire, too? Are we going to have a weenie roast over the fucking engine?"

Roberto sniffed. "I don't smell anything."

Silver got out of the car, pissed that something was wrong with his ride. He cussed as he raised the hood of the car. What he looked at was caked oil and dirt on the manifold and an engine whirling warm air into his face. He swept leaves stacked like cards in the hollow between the battery and the wheel well.

"There's something over there." Roberto had one hand shading his brow and the other pointing.

Silver turned. Three people were pointing from the top of the three-tiered Hink's garage. Behind them, a huge black cloud unfurled and ash floated on the hot wind. Silver slapped at a speck of wayward ash and crumbled it in his palm. He sniffed it, nose pulsating, and remarked after close study, "That's wood."

"What's wood?" Roberto asked.

He shoved his palm toward Roberto's nose. "It smells like potato chips to me."

Silver parked the car and figured that if he couldn't get it started again, the city could have it. With Roberto in tow, the two climbed the parking structure, where curious onlookers stood. One person had a set of binoculars, the ground lenses reflecting leaping flames. A child was taking a picture with a disposable camera.

"*Híjole.*" Silver whistled.

In the Oakland hills, a fire raged. The flames were tall as trees and were, in fact, devouring trees along with homes and unlucky deer who made their living eating flowers from the backyards of these homes. Smoke billowed. Smoke swallowed sunlight and the flight of birds. Smoke tainted the already dirty air. A helicopter hovered, and sirens of fire engines and cruisers tore up the silence.

"It looks hot!" Roberto hollered over the sirens. "You think it can come over here?"

Silver remained mute. He had worked as a firefighter in Yolo County when he was nineteen. He was familiar with smoke and fire and how soon deer, possum, raccoons, squirrels, and feral cats would rush from those hills. Mice would follow at the last moment. The dumbest of dogs—Irish setters and springer spaniels—would wear a coat of flames and try to lick them like wounds. But the cockroaches, immigrant insects in black shiny armor, would scamper for cooler ground.

"It's our lucky day," Silver forecasted after he caught another black ash in his hand. He smudged the ash into his palm. Happily he felt a poem coming on with the first line: "Flames live in the eyes of rascals and three-legged dogs." He felt like singing the line, but instead he clutched the rail of the top floor of Hink's garage.

"Come on," he told Roberto. He hurried down the stairwell with Roberto asking where they were going, and why.

Silver and Roberto pushed the Honda into Hiro's gas station and paid up front for a new alternator. While the citizens of Oakland swarmed like ants toward the fire, eating houses large as estates, Silver was feeling mighty fortunate. The sun was eclipsed in the smothering smoke. They listened to the small radio Hiro had propped on the counter. The reports said that the fire had started the night before, smoldered, and come back to life.

"We're going to make some money," Silver informed Roberto.

After the alternator was installed, the two drove to the McDonald's on University Avenue. They ate in a greasy booth, stabbing their french fries into a blob of ketchup pooled on the plastic foam shell. As they ate, Silver, hot with his own fire, started a poem on the back of an envelope, then moved his verse to a McDonald's bag on the second revision:

> Shadows crept over the old man's face.
> He lurched for that blackness
> And caught only air. No, he caught
> An ash that could have been, yes, his *vieja*,
> Gone for good. The old man cried,
> Where is she! Where am I without her!

Roberto observed this knee-swaying revelry of Silver's. He chewed the burnt and bitter ends of leftover french fries. He remarked that he never knew a poet, at which Silver chuckled and laughed. "You're a lucky bastard."

Without being encouraged, Silver read the poem aloud and waited for a response. When one didn't come forth, he asked, "So what do you think?" He threw a burnt fry into his mouth, then wet a finger and dabbed at the salt on the peeled-open bag.

"That's sad," Roberto responded after a momentary look of confusion. "The poor guy's wife is dead and he has to hang in there."

Silver's face brightened. He was beginning to like Roberto more and more. He even schooled his friend on a major point regarding verse. "You got to make your poem dark!" He mulled over his assertion, tumbling ice cubes like dice in his mouth. "Nah, not dark, but *muy triste*. Or otherwise people will think you're *gavacho* just like them. You know, people with jobs and shit."

"I thought poetry had to sound pretty," Roberto said.

Silver tossed his balled napkin into the mouth of the paper bag. He snarled, "Nah, homes, you got it wrong. It's got to sound like you're nowhere, like you're down and out. *Entiendes?*" His leg twitched and his balled fist rolled with sweat, a sensation he experienced when he was in the mood for writing. He studied the first poem he had written in months, his words surmounting grease, salt, and the scent of burgers. He ripped his poem from the McDonald's bag, stuffed it in his back pocket, and said, "We're out of here."

From a filthy phone booth, Silver called J. J. Albert, the PI, whose number was in the yellow pages and, to Silver's surprise, circled with a pen. Seemed like business just rolled J. J.'s way. The man answered on the third ring.

"Yeah," J. J. answered.

"Silver Mendez," Silver said huskily. He had to meet J. J. on his own terms—bad. "You seen the fire, ain't you?"

"Not only did I see it, I smelled it and tasted it, and it burned my goddamn house down!" J. J. answered hotly, his anger blowing through the crosstown wires and heating up Silver's ear. "Now, who in the fuck are you?"

"Friend of Miguel's."

Silver explained that Miguel had taught him a few tricks of the insurance trade and now, with houses burning to their foundations, insurance companies would want videos of the damage. Hell, Silver told J. J., with the camera he had on his shoulder, they could make enough money to gas up every Cadillac he owned in the past and the ones to come.

"Motherfucker!" J. J. yelled. "I don't drive me no niggah car! I got me a Mercedes." More hot anger blew through the wires for a steady minute before he stopped to catch his breath.

"You know what I mean," Silver countered, slightly wilted from the barrage of words. The fact that he didn't know how to load a video camera made him nervous enough, but to reduce his future boss to a Cadillac man was plain wrong. He decided to keep such prejudices to poetry.

"Nah, you get what I mean!" J. J. hollered. "You calling from a pay phone. I can hear those cars in the back. How many people work from a pay phone? You answer me that! What kinda low-class clown going to call me, J. J. Albert, black businessman of the year two years in a row in Alameda County, from a mother-fuckin' pay phone? I bet you at McDonald's."

Silver glanced at the Golden Arches, where a gang of pigeons huddled close enough to play poker. He considered the debris at his feet, where spilled french fries lay. He crushed a single fry to paste.

"Listen, J. J., me and—," Silver started.

"Nah, you listen, buddy. I got enough people around me to meet my needs. People I know. People who got offices to make their calls. You know what I mean?"

"But I'm a poet," Silver argued. "A poet can see the damage others can't."

"What the fuck does that mean?" J. J. laughed. His laughter was more hurtful than his anger. J. J. said he knew a black poet who hung himself in a garage in St. Louis. He suggested that Silver do the same thing and pronto.

Silver hung up.

"What did he say?" Roberto asked.

"The guy's hard to reach. I'm surprised he's in business."

Silver was still not discouraged. His eyes floated skyward to ash parachuting in abundance from the Oakland hills fire. There was a helicopter circling, and sirens had made dogs hoarse from Berkeley to Hayward. They were wailing to the moon, but no moon stood in the sky.

"I don't get it," Roberto said.

Silver was increasingly doubtful of Roberto, who seemed to Silver light-headed in his simpleness, or perhaps from the lack of oxygen that the fire was snatching from the air. Silver tried again. He said that their new business—he the photographer and Roberto a security guard kind of guy—would document burned houses. Owners would pay good money, Silver reasoned, as there was money in ash and people's sorrows. He made this remark and thought that perhaps he could weave it into a poem later. For now, he had to get to work.

They drove to Miguel's house. While Roberto hunched over to pat and speak to the grave of his pup, Master, dead no more than a few days, Silver called Miguel to the window.

"Buzz me up," Silver requested.

"*No puedo*, homes," Miguel answered. "I'm busy." He explained that the phone had been ringing off the hook. He had so much work as a consequence of the fire that he had brought in college help.

"I can help, too," Silver said hopefully.

Miguel shook his head. "Nah, I got enough people. You won't do."

"I thought you were my friend," Silver said.

"Come on, Silver!" Miguel scolded. "Be honest with yourself!" His mouth bunched up, like he was holding back water, and then spat out, "Your days are over! You're a loser!"

The wind of the brutal and unforgivable attack rocked Silver back on his heels.

"That's what you think of me?" Silver stepped back to get a better view of Miguel in his loft. But he couldn't handle the view of Miguel, three flights up surrounded by nice furniture and the sound of a cellular phone ringing, while he, a once famous poet, was in the street standing next to Roberto, a homeless guy patting the grave of a dog. Silver wheeled around without hearing the answer, though he did make out Miguel shutting his window. The window was closed for good.

Silver and Roberto sat in the car, which faced his former mattress. Two others were sleeping in their spot, both of them shirtless, their ribs ladders for the flies of a late summer morning. Neither was aware of the fire that had erupted in the Oakland hills. Neither probably remembered his own name, seeing that they were burned out on drugs and not ever coming back. Their own fire had come and gone.

"We'll just go up there ourselves," Silver said. He liked the ring of the words and wrote them down on a notepad. It sounded biblical, he thought—Moses on the mountain with a blazing stare and a beard as long as a cape.

Silver believed he could make something of the situation. He didn't strike the match or flick the cigarette out a car window. He was blameless for the burning of the best part of Oakland. All the poor people in the flatlands raised their heads to their successful brothers and sisters living in the hills. Some perhaps taunted those professionals, and others gasped at the ferocity of the fire lighting up the sky. Others were perhaps thinking of what to steal. No, Silver figured, he didn't create that fire. He was too busy trying to spark his own career back to life.

He drove to the Salvation Army and bought the newest-looking 35-mm camera in the glass case, then two rolls of film from Long's Drugs. They drove in the direction of the fire, stopping at the Claremont Hotel, where the street was closed and hundreds of people milled, struck up friendships, and waited for the fire to creep down the street like lava. Two cops were directing traffic, and two other cops were pushing people around for the fun of it. Silver had been stomped by the police in the past, and usually after the first six or seven footfalls from their black boots, the pain was an unfortunate jostle. He kept his distance, as did Roberto, who started wailing about his six months at Santa Rita jail.

"I already heard your story, dude!" Silver snarled at Roberto.

Roberto hung his head.

"Hey, I'm sorry, but you've already told me." Silver reached for Roberto's shoulder, but his friend swung away, a dead man twisting on his own private gallows.

Fumbling for change in his pocket, Silver bought two chocolate ice creams from a smart street vendor, an old Chinese man with a white paper hat down around his eyes. They ate the ice cream and watched the fire blaze orange behind the trees. Roberto crowed between licks that he liked chocolate but strawberry was

111

his favorite flavor. He hushed up when he realized that his comment sounded like a childish complaint.

A deer with nubby antlers emerged from the smoke and stopped in the middle of the road to eye the crowd, who cooed tender words and finger-snapped for the deer to come and be rescued. Its wet nose pulsated, its ribs rose and fell, and its dark eyes were alive with the turning red lights of the idling police car. The deer scanned the crowd, stepping backward on hooves sharp as flint. It turned and pranced back into the smoke. Survival was likelier among fire and smoke than among people for whom meat and destruction were primary concerns.

Since they couldn't get around the barricades, Silver suggested that they go to the downtown public library. They drove to downtown Berkeley and read magazines until Silver saw the high windows darken and a single star appear.

"Let's go," Silver told Roberto, who was reading an aviation magazine. He had both hands on the magazine as if he were flying it.

From there they drove to Passo Coffee House in Oakland. It was open mike for poetry night.

A veteran in the poetry scene, Silver had gone through several seasons of reading his poems in public. Often he read only parts of them. He would then ask the audience of other poets, plus an occasional Spanish-speaking busboy, where the next part should lead. How do you think this poem is going to end? he would ask with a hand in his hair, a poetic touch. He did this bantering for a laugh, he recalled, but stopped it when an elderly woman poet with stringy hair said the poem should end in the garbage can followed by his own skinny ass. He would have had it out with her, but she had three books to her credit and an honest literary award of two hundred and fifty dollars. That counted for something back in the midseventies.

Silver thought there was a chance that he would run into a friend or a friend of a friend. And who knows, he figured, perhaps two frisky gals would latch onto them. It didn't matter. He and Roberto needed a place to throw their bones, even if they were under a tree in someone's yard. With any luck, they could get to sleep on a carpeted floor or a couch and have free reign of the bathroom—he now smelled an onion simmering in the juices of his own wet armpits. You got to do something, he mulled. His mind was nimble with options.

"You're going to like this, homes," Silver told Roberto.

"But I don't know too many words," Roberto admitted.

"I told you, man, poetry is about feeling sad." Silver turned over his definition of poetry like a wishbone in his mouth. He swallowed the bone with only a mild scratch of hurt. "Yeah, it's about loneliness and things not working out."

"I don't want to be sad no more. I want to try some other feelings." Roberto placed an elbow out the window and swung his face away, his hair flicking in the wind.

Silver felt for his friend. He pounded a gentle fist against his shoulder. "Don't worry, we'll try other emotions. But in time."

The café was busy with the flash of forks and knives. Chairs scraped against the floor. Steam rose from gourmet burgers and curly fries. A pizza as a large as bike wheel sat among loud college students. Their hands grappled for a slice, and Silver considered moving close by and throwing his own hands among the ruckus. Who would notice? he asked himself.

Silver could spot other poets waiting for the paying clients to clear out. These poets were sitting before empty latte cups, the foam licked clean. One poet was wetting his whistle with a glass of water with no ice. A toothpick was shoved in the corner of his mouth.

What meat did he eat, Silver thought, but his own words? He liked that notion and wrote it down on a piece of paper.

"Are you writing a poem?" Roberto asked. He pushed his head over Silver's shoulder, snatching a peek. "I thought you were supposed to sit down to write."

Silver ignored Roberto. He felt happy when he finished jotting down his thought, folded it neatly, and placed it in his shirt pocket. "It's too early to go in." He didn't want to be seated, drink his coffee, and have nothing to peer into but its grounds or Roberto's sad face.

They stood outside, leaning against the wall. Neither said anything. Finally Silver asked, "How come you're always holding your stomach?"

"I hurt it. I swallowed a piece of metal."

Silver prompted him to flesh out his story.

"I was a security guard, like I told you, but before that, man, I worked in a factory and this shaving flew up from the lathe and right into my mouth." He made a small circling motion with his fingers. "It was like a noodle. You know, kind of curly."

"No shit?"

Roberto rubbed his stomach. "Yeah, but I know it's still there. I'm going to die with it."

Sirens wailed in the murky distance of nightfall, but the dogs, silenced by their hoarseness or the beatings from their owners, had stopped barking. A car idled at a red light with the radio blaring. The news reported that six people had been confirmed dead in the fire, sixty-two injured, and hundreds of houses burned or burning. The fire department promised that the fire would be contained by midnight or early morning at the latest. Governor Wilson had declared Oakland a disaster area, and an angry Oakland mayor vouched to get to the bottom of the fire—find out who in the hell was responsible. All this was picked up within thirty seconds. Despite the horrific events, Silver saw the charred ruins as the promised land. He saw money. He saw a fire melting the gold goblets of the rich and rivulets racing to the poor in

114

the flatlands of Oakland. If he had been religious, Silver would have dropped to his knees and praised God.

"I don't like fires," Roberto stated. He recalled for Silver how he had once burned his Christmas tree to see what would happen. He was eight, bored, and sidelined with rickets because he hadn't been getting enough to eat.

"What happened?"

"My mom cried," Roberto said, his own eyes stung with this recollection. "She cried because she knew I was sick but still needed a whipping because I had to learn to be a good kid."

Silver chewed the inside of his cheek pensively. He asked, "What's rickets like?"

"It's like walking on stilts. You got no balance because your bones are weak."

Silver rifled through his pockets. He had three dollars and dirt-caked change—one quarter had dark grime around Washington's eyes that made him look as if he were wearing sunglasses. He counted the money in his palm, then shoved it back into his pocket in time to acknowledge a poet friend.

"I'll see you inside, bro," Silver told the poet, who held the door open for his girl. She sported cropped hair. Earrings and knobs dangled from her ears like wind chimes.

"You like girls like that?" Roberto whispered.

Silver remained silent.

"You do like girls, don't you?" Roberto asked, worry in his voice.

"You know I do. But I like mine with hair."

The two went back into the café. They took a seat in the back, where other poets sat, their manuscripts flipped open.

Silver pulled from his coat pocket his book *Tigres en Armas.* It was bent and spotted with the leprosy of previous readings. He thumbed it once and then gave it to Roberto. "Choose a poem for me."

Roberto accepted the slim book and turned it from front to back and from top to bottom, unsure what to do.

"Open it up and look, dude!" Silver laughed from his belly but stopped laughing when Roberto suggested that he read the table of contents.

"Man, that ain't a poem! It's the table of contents. What's wrong with you?" Silver was aware of what was wrong: Roberto was uneducated. Silver decided that he was going to see that the spaces in Roberto's thinking were filled.

Roberto asked what he meant by the "table of contents."

"It's a list of the poems!" He shook his head and muttered, "*Ay, Chihuahua!* We got to work on you." Silver got up, ordered two lattes, and returned to his table, walking slowly. He didn't intend to spill a single drop.

He sat down in time for the first poet to come up and recite a poem by memory. He did this with his eyes closed. It was about an elephant who loses its memory but finds it when it drinks from a watering hole where crocodiles gather.

"In African mythology, crocodiles are not only a symbol of death and darkness but also memory. Thus, in my poem the elephant forgets but finally regains its memory by drinking from the waters of remembrance." The poet beamed at his friends at his own table.

Silver bent his head toward Roberto. "That is a crock of shit. Crocodiles, my ass."

"But I like crocodiles," said Roberto.

"That's not the point." Silver sipped his latte, foam clinging like suds to his beard. He licked the suds. "The poet is a phony who ain't yet lived. Why go all the way to Africa? This dude should stick around Oakland."

Roberto lowered his face.

"Aw, man, I didn't mean to get down on you." He touched Roberto's sleeve. "I like crocodiles, too." He sat up in his chair.

"In fact, I had a cousin who got bit by an alligator. It wasn't a crocodile, but who cares when you got thirty teeth tearing your arm to pieces."

A poet with long hair next jumped up and rushed to the front. Smiling, he said he was going to read a poem about the Oakland fire. He said the poem was called "Resilience" and dedicated to his friend's mother, whose house would have burned except it was miles from the center of the fire. The poem offered the sound effects of fire, gushing water from a fire hose, and a siren that would have brought a dog howling if there had been one present. As he moved toward the finale, the young poet brought out a cigarette lighter and flicked it to life. He exited by mimicking an old lady running from flames.

Roberto applauded.

Not wishing to deflate his friend's feelings, Silver clapped and nodded. "Good stuff," he concluded falsely.

The next poet read a sectioned poem about her cat named Jewel. Then she read a poem about her dog Laurel, also sectioned and longer than a feature-length film.

"Shit," Silver muttered to himself after he swirled his tongue in his empty coffee cup. "She'll be reading a poem about her goldfish next."

The goldfish poem, to Silver's surprise, followed, but first the poet defined a pet as an animal who responds to your feelings. The goldfish, she argued, was not a pet because it responded only to fish flakes. In a near whisper she read a portion of the poem, then stopped to remind the audience that her goldfish was nameless, and wasn't it remarkable that such a creature existed in a society that depended on names and brand names. But someone from the audience challenged her by saying that in fourteenth-century China wild animals were sometimes given proper names.

The poet countered, "Now, what do we really mean by wild? The panda has claws, but would you consider that wonderful animal wild? The panda is known to cuddle a broken branch." She pulled her hair behind her ear, glowing. "In China during that period there was a connection of humans to nature, a state that we have sorely lost. Consider the artwork."

If he had been stronger, Silver would have crushed his coffee cup in his bare hands.

"In the artwork, especially in the Tang period," the poet continued, "you'll notice that the doors to their homes slide open, while in Western civilization they what?" She scanned her audience before summing up, " . . . They close."

"That's stupid gibberish," Silver growled, louder than he intended. A few people swiveled their attention toward his table. Since all knew where the comment had arisen, he volunteered his own feelings. "Okay, I'm wild, and I ain't got a name in poetry or nowhere! Am I an animal, then? Is that how it is? Am I a creature in my own nameless society?"

The poet considered Silver languidly for a moment and then turned to the other poet, dismissing Silver with a sigh that was from her throat and not deep down. "Yes, I have read that in China—"

Silver stood up. "Hey, don't do that to me!"

The poet turned her large, luminous eyes on him. She looked like Venus rising from her shell, but with smaller breasts. "Excuse me, but you're being rude."

Roberto started to get up to leave, but Silver pulled him back into his chair. To the poet, he shouted, "And that's the worst you can find in me?" He pointed at his own chest. "I'm rude."

"No, you're rudely wrong." She now moved from the stool back to her table.

Rudely wrong, Silver thought. What does that mean? He turned the phrase over and when he couldn't fathom its meaning, he shouted, "China! Africa! Crocodiles and elephants! And about that old lady whose house almost burned down! What do you know about pain! I bet she was a Republican!" His fiery gaze could have torched the poets and the dishwasher who had stopped to adjust his hair net and listen. Some looked away, mildly frightened, and two giggled and clinked their coffee cups as in a toast. "What are you grinning at?" he asked them.

"A bum," the young man answered. "A rudely wrong bum."

There was that phrase again! Silver snorted and sat back down.

Roberto pulled on Silver's sleeve. "Let's go. I don't like poetry."

Silver slapped Roberto's hand away.

"I'm a bum. I'm a crocodile, too!" He pressed his hands together and opened and closed them, snapping them together like jaws.

"Hey, man, we're just listening to poetry," the young man started. "What's your problem?"

"My problem is that I don't care for goldfish in poetry. I come in and buy a coffee for me and a bud here and we have to listen to that shit."

"I like it," the young man countered.

"Good for you. But let me tell you that poetry is about people who suffer. Do you know what that means?" Silver shared his sneer with everyone in the café, including the manager, who had come out of the kitchen with a towel over his shoulder. His hands were propped on his hips.

To the young man, Silver hollered, "I bet you got a nice family and all that."

"That's right," the young man said. "My mom and dad are together and I got a girl that I like. What of it?"

"Family values and shit! Fake poetry! You'll find out!"

The young man got up, walked up slowly to Silver, and stated flatly that the poems he himself wrote were true.

Silver huffed.

"And this . . . ," the young man said, winding up a punch from which there was no escape because Silver was in his late thirties and terribly slow, "is also true."

Silver was rocked on his heels by a blow right between his eyes, which were already letting go of their anger and getting ready for pain. He staggered into the arms of the manager, who dabbed Silver's face with his towel.

After the young man left with his friend and Silver staggered to his feet, Roberto said, "I didn't know poets could hit that hard."

They slept that night in the car. The next morning Silver woke with his eyes swollen. He slurped what he thought was blood, but was only the sour residue of his latte and stomach acids. He eyed the rearview mirror. From all appearances, he was hung over. He was glad, however, to see that the dye on his face was fading and his usual sallow color was returning. He wanted to get back to normal.

"How do I look?" Silver asked.

Roberto avoided Silver's eyes.

Silver returned for a second glance in the rearview mirror. It had been several years since he had gotten into a fight. But what had occurred last night was nothing like a fight. It was a single blow and all because—the phrase stuck—he was "rudely wrong." He closed his eyes and recalled his last confrontation—what stupidity!—over a chair at a party. He had left to take a leak, and when he returned, a guy with combed hair and ironed jeans was sitting in his place. Silver told him to get out of *his* chair or he would open a can of whip ass on him. Little did Silver know that the guy was a student of a kung fu master from the iron fist system.

They drove to a Denny's on Telegraph Avenue, and with the rattling change in his pockets Silver ordered two coffees. They drank their coffees greedily, used the rest room in turns, and left with their bellies sloshing.

"What are we going to do now?" Roberto asked as he buckled

up in the Honda. "I'm hungry. Everyone's eating but us." He looked over his shoulder and surveyed the backseat, crammed with Silver's belongings. "Maybe we can sell some of your stuff." He picked up a cup and studied it. "If you got a set like this, we probably could make maybe two dollars."

Silver ignored Roberto's suggestion. He appraised a morning sky that was grayish near the bay but orangish against the eastern hills. There was smoke in the sky, but the heavy layer of yesterday had broken apart and had sunk to the ground in the form of soot. He was thinking of the old woman's house that almost burned. There had to be other old women up there, scared, possibly injured, and wanting to be saved even by the lowly likes of the homeless.

Roberto glanced up where Silver was looking. "What's up there?"

"The hills, dude."

They drove toward the Claremont Hotel. Although the fire had been contained during the night, Ashby Avenue was still blocked off with wooden barricades. A fire engine was stationed there along with a few cops. The ice cream vendor was also there, leaning on his cart and waiting for business. The fire engine idled, its hoses fat with water and ready to douse the flames if they should reignite and spill into Berkeley. Silver kicked one of the hoses with the tip of his shoe. He wished he could drink from that pulsating hose, one drink so powerful that his thirst would be quenched for the rest of his life.

Silver returned to his car for the camera, which he shoved in his jacket. He walked up to one of the officers.

"Hey, I got to get the stuff out of my house." He pointed vaguely at the hills.

The cop turned and sized up Silver, from his worn shoes to his bulbous nose. "What's your address?"

Silver stalled, tongue heavy as a metal latch. "That's a sort of personal question."

The officer stepped toward Silver, gravel grinding like bones under his boots. He stabbed a finger close to Silver's chest. "If I find your ass up there, you're going to be arrested." His breath gave off the scent of a full breakfast.

Silver walked away, only slightly daunted. "What an asshole," he muttered to himself.

"What did he say?" Roberto asked.

"The dude said it's cool," Silver lied. He told Roberto that the officer permitted their entry as long as they went by the side street. The officer didn't want to encourage foot traffic.

They cut through the parking lot of the Claremont Hotel and over a ten-foot chain-link fence. They found themselves in a backyard where a dog was pawing a yellow tennis ball. The dog barked playfully at them, wagged its tail, and picked up the tennis ball.

"Not now, dude," Silver said.

Still, the dog approached with the ball in its mouth. Silver took the ball and hurled it in the far corner of the yard. While the dog chased after it, they made their way out of the yard, down the side of the house, and toward the sidewalk and onto Ashby Avenue. Half hidden behind a sycamore, Silver spied the cops and the idling fire engine.

"Why are we hiding?" Roberto asked from behind Silver.

"Practice," Silver answered. He started climbing up the hill with Roberto following.

"I don't get what we're doing," Roberto whined after two blocks. He was out of breath and holding his stomach.

"We're going to look around, dude. Be like tourists, you know." He admitted that the insurance thing was plain dumb, but with the fire having eaten away at the rich people's homes, someone somewhere needed their help. They could move furniture out of houses, cut down a tree that had fallen over the roof, or aid an old guy dying. Silver confessed that he would never go through a dying person's pocket, but if such a person's last words were, "Here, take my wallet," he would consider it a sort of communion between the living and the dead. Silver reminded Roberto that they had to remain upbeat.

"I don't want to see no one dying," Roberto cried. "How are we going to make money? I'm hungry. I just don't get it."

"You don't have to get it. You just got to do what there is to do." Silver didn't know what he meant by his remark, but it sounded like the poetry of a Super Bowl commercial.

Their walk up the hill was poetry, too, with the scuttling leaves blowing in the hot wind and birds black as charcoal scolding them from the telephone wires. He had never read more than three pages of Dante's *Inferno*, but he was aware that what happened to the dude in the poem was not unlike his own trail toward redemption. Silver figured that he was walking toward something meaningful. He expected to behold an incident to later get drunk over and repeat until his friends told to him to shut up.

A cop car roared down Ashby, and the cop eyed them through the smudged windshield but didn't brake. The car seemed to be in a hurry, almost reckless on squealing tires.

"We're going to get in trouble," Roberto whined. "I don't want to go back to Santa Rita!"

Silver pretended not to hear his friend, seating himself on a low wooden fence to catch his breath. He wished he had a cup of coffee and a sandwich. When he touched his stomach, he swore that he could almost feel his spine, the vertebrae stacked like dominoes. He angled his face toward his armpits: the onions buried in his flesh would scare a skunk into a river. He smelled alive.

"We're untouchable, dude," Silver said after a moment of rest. "Who can hurt us? I can even see better in both my eyes."

Roberto leaned his face toward Silver's ragged face. "Yeah, they do look better, huh?"

They climbed Ashby Avenue toward Highway 13, which was

empty except for the shell of a burned-out car. Silver inspected the driver's side with its seat cremated to wire and metal springs. The dash was melted, and the steering wheel had the shape of a hangman's noose. Silver took a picture of the car. He next asked Roberto to take a picture of him and the car. He climbed into the driver's seat and smiled.

After that they crossed the highway, slapping away the smoke from their faces, and picked up tree limbs to use as canes. They were now walking uphill, both of them coughing and sneezing. They stopped to take a picture of a family of deer, none of them hurt, with their heads poking around a burned bush.

Through the smoke, they made out two firemen whacking the flames with shovels. To Silver, they looked like astronauts with oxygen tanks on their backs and masks on their faces.

Quickly Roberto fell behind, his complaining voice now lost in the sirens, the buzzing of planes with their fire-retardant loads, and the chewing sound of fire eating homes and trees. Near the reservoir, the fire had bucked up, once again burning.

Silver mulled over Roberto's complaint. Just what were they doing in the closed-off area? Instinct drove him to kick among the ruins for something divergent from his usual routine—lately, sleeping in his car or on a thin mattress in a public place. He also knew that people were locked in their homes, confused and helpless, and if he could find someone in more than chaos than his own life, he could become something of a hero. Perhaps something fine and lasting would result. His own poetry had been anything but fine and lasting.

After a killer hike up Terrace Avenue, Silver stopped to catch his breath and wait up for Roberto. He squeezed his eyes closed, saw an orange light behind his eyelids, and then touched his tender nose. When he opened his eyes, he saw a raccoon scamper past with its back singed and smoking. The raccoon made its way under a fence and disappeared.

"Poor dude," Silver said.

Roberto finally appeared, eating an apple.

"Where did you get that?" Silver asked. His own hunger was tearing at the sides of his stomach, gnawing at the fat that he had hoped to deploy for strength in the coming winter.

Roberto told Silver that he had gotten it from a tree. He polished another apple on the front of his pants and tossed it to Silver.

Silver remarked that he was more thirsty than hungry.

"Apples got water," Roberto said. "I read that apples and nectarines and fruit like that are ninety-seven percent water."

"I don't see no faucets on them," Silver said snidely, then laughed until he coughed. Still, he bit into the apple and ate it to its bitter core. He informed Roberto that he still had dye on his face.

Roberto touched his cheek, then brought his hand away and studied his fingertips.

"Hey, man, let me take your picture. You look good against those hills."

Roberto took a peep over his shoulder. The background was burned hills the color of a German shepherd's snout. He wiggled his mouth into a smile when Silver said, "*Queso.*"

They climbed up Moraga Avenue and walked among the ruins of shriveled gardens and burned houses, the windows blown out and the roofs smoldering. Cars and motorcycles were gutted, and a motor home was twisted metal and still ticking from the heat. The fire department had given up on that street. The blaze had even bent the street sign. It had split the asphalt and left the trees like burned matches, the tips smoking.

"There's a cop over there!" Roberto's voice was full of panic.

Three cops and a fireman poked around a garage that was still intact, while the house, once big as a barn, had burned to the rough framing. Two houses away, a television crew was taking live scenes.

"Be cool. They can't see us," Silver remarked. "Anyhow, we're citizens of the U.S. of A."

They cut a path through singed oleanders and up a public stairwell, careful not to touch the steel rails, which he knew were hot. They walked a circling mile through the twisting neighborhood until they came upon an enclave of homes that had escaped the fire. Some of the home owners were in their yards, soaking bushes with garden hoses and sweeping the sidewalks of ash. Others were standing with their hands on their hips, assessing the destroyed homes at the end of the block.

"We can clean this up, huh, Silver?"

Silver agreed. He agreed that they could probably start anywhere but warned Roberto that they had to work for serious money. "At least eight dollars an hour! I'm sorry that their homes burned and shit, but we got to live, too." He was committed to work and to a new life in which he would have the free time to study the blisters on his palms. Forget poetry, he told Roberto. He balled his hand into a fist, but it quickly unrolled into lanky fingers.

They came upon a woman crying on the steps of her house, which was dark from smoke but otherwise intact. She was in her bathrobe. Her hair was wild and her eyes were even wilder when she brought her hands from her face. Tears flooded the lines on her cheeks.

"My cat's dead," she remarked when they got closer.

The dead cat lay stretched like a beaver pelt behind her on the steps and appeared to be bathing itself in the morning sunlight. To Silver, the cat looked like it might roll over, raise itself up, arch its back, and meow for a plate of milk.

"What happened?" Silver asked lamely.

The woman shook her head. A single earring jingled a tinny music.

Silver thought of saying that they could bury her pet for a couple of dollars but held his tongue in his mouth. He approached the woman even closer and observed the gray line in her parted and dyed hair. Her hands were wrinkled and her bare feet nearly blue with bulging veins.

Roberto stood back, biting a fingernail.

"Ma'am, I could take a picture of your cat." Silver risked this request and risked putting his hand on her shoulder when she started to cry loudly. "Ma'am, I didn't mean that. I thought you would just like to see a picture of . . ." Silver wished a tree would fall and strike him dead.

Her bawling jerked her shoulders up and down. A single tear fell between her feet. When she moved her hands from her face, more tears fell. She wiped her eyes, sighing deeply. She studied Silver after her crying simmered to sniffles. She dabbed her nostrils with a crushed Kleenex.

"Did you get hurt in the fire?" she asked "Your face is red."

Silver skated his fingertips over his brow. "No, ma'am, I just look this way." He contorted his answer even further. "It's dye from where me and Roberto worked at." His eyes roamed over the memory of yesterday's scuffle at the café. "Plus someone hit me yesterday."

Roberto nodded. "It's true, ma'am." He told her that Silver said that poetry should be sad, but he didn't believe him until the young man knocked Silver into the arms of the manager.

"You're a poet?" the woman asked.

Silver nodded, too.

The woman swallowed. She turned stiffly and ran her hand through her cat's fur. Silver was struck by how the cat was cleaner than either he or Roberto. They were like walking rags with human heat rising from their skin and bones. And surely they knew more than "meow," but at the moment Silver was so thirsty for water or watered-down milk that he would have meowed if asked. He licked his lips and remained quiet before making an offer to bury the cat. "Me and my friend will do it for you."

Silver searched the yard for a shovel and returned to the woman, who was now standing, her bathrobe tied but flapping in the wind.

"Everything's going to be okay," Silver comforted. "We'll bury your cat, and if you got work for us, we would be grateful. We're here to help." He stared at Roberto, waiting for him to speak up.

"That's right, ma'am. Me and Silver can do anything you want. We can wash your house down. Get rid of the smoke."

The woman raked her hand over her eyes.

"My cat's name is Dover."

Silver regarded the cat before allowing the woman privacy to speak to her cat for the last time. The two walked away and scanned the yard for a grave for the cat.

Silver had seen poorly scrawled signs that said Will Work for Food. Now he was beginning to believe in them. Testing the hardness of the ground, he raised a shovel and jabbed it into the earth, which was surprisingly moist in spite of the fire that rolled over the land. He thought of the cat's death and his own eventual death. His own plot would be easy to dig because a small tractor would do the work. The hard part would be finding friends to carry him to his resting place. He had been dying for years, dying through poetry that didn't work for him or the ears it fell on. Now it was time to use his body to get by in life.

Silver chose a spot near a rosebush whose roots, he imagined, would feast on the spoils of the cat. He raised the shovel and dug a hole that could hold a larger animal, a deer or raccoon, and broke a sweat that he first thought was rain. He shaded his eyes, regarded the sky, and saw only the ring of a glaring sun. When he looked back at the porch, he saw that the woman was gone, perhaps inside her house.

He returned to the steps of the porch, picked up the cat, already stiff, and brought it to its grave. He placed Dover in the grave, politely crossed its legs left over right, and, impulsively, rang the bell on its collar. He remembered that he had climbed into the Oakland hills in search of something new to do, something fine and lasting. Whether this burial was fine, he wasn't sure because he had no prayer to offer to the cat's god. But he was convinced that once you descended into the earth, your time there—through rain or snow, or the roll of fire—would last longer than the icy light of stars in the godless sky.

The Untimely Passing of the Clock Radio

For nineteen years, Gustavo Hernandez stood in front of the Walnut Bank and paced three steps in one direction, only to turn and pace in the other direction. Known as Gus to the tellers and customers, he marked time since he was in no hurry. He was a patient and responsible man waiting for retirement, his patience a sort of gift for not wanting much from life. Still, this pacing added mileage to his feet, more than he had logged in riding buses and trains from Monterrey, Mexico, to the duplex apartment in Oakland where he now lived. He performed his routine without complaint, even if the customers had money and he had almost none. You get what luck brings you, he supposed, and didn't hold any bitterness toward people with more than him. His job was to protect what was theirs.

Originally there had been two security guards, but with the decline of downtown business and the installation of cameras that eyeballed everyone's movements, including Gus's pacing, a position was eliminated. This had occurred four years ago, a blink of time, Gus figured. The other security guard left clutching an envelope of severance pay, arm in arm with a drunk and staggering *compadre*.

"It's all yours, *viejo*," Roberto, a young Chicano with no respect for his task, had taunted as he stripped off the jacket of his uniform. He threw this jacket at Gus, who caught it as if it were a baby.

Gus couldn't grasp this young man's happiness in leaving. It's not a great job, he knew, but still, a job was a job. He sensed disloyalty in Roberto's voice and even observed a sneer in the corner of his mouth. Now, that's too much, Gus had thought. He noticed that Roberto didn't look back even once as he and his friend crowed loudly and took turns slapping each other playfully with the envelope of money. Roberto disappeared around the corner and out of his life, a mere specter that occasionally floated across his eyes when he was in bed.

Gus was not more than five-foot six, and now, at fifty-nine, he was shrinking in his pigeon gray uniform. He had stood in one place so long—on a walkway between two cement planter boxes— that the vertebrae of his spine had begun to collapse, grinding down like teeth. And although Gus didn't mind his job, he wanted to be done with his years as a security guard, finish them before his uniform became a huge floppy tent over his body. He had only two weeks to retirement.

His days had been eventless, and he was thankful for that. Just to stand for seven hours and smile occasionally at customers, just to open a door for a hobbling older man or woman, or just to glide a wheelchair effortlessly into the lobby. He gave directions to lost souls. He watered the lung-shaped plants in the planter boxes and swiped candy and gum wrappers that scurried across the sidewalk. He pulled back the cuff of his uniform jacket and read the time, usually in Spanish, to passersby. His life involved simply pacing from one place to another, a traction of years.

Only twice had Gus faced danger. He was younger then, stronger, and, in his mind, as bold as a real policeman. He had to wrestle with a bank robber one morning on July 17, 1986. Gus was surprised by his instincts, surprised that he had the presence of mind to trip and bury the knife blade of his elbow into this scoundrel. The blow landed hard enough that the robber's eyeglasses flew off his face, a gush of pain issuing from his mouth. Now and then, in the secrecy of his apartment, Gus rubbed his left elbow, cherished it for its action some eleven years before.

Then, on November 16, 1995, the eleventh anniversary of his position with the bank, he talked a woman out of jumping from the roof. The woman had threatened to jump after her husband had withdrawn their life's savings, that is, everything except twenty-three dollars, the sum of their married years. Distraught, she sat on the edge of the roof. But he coaxed her back by reminding her that life was much more precious than money, infinitely more meaningful than a husband who would run away with another woman. Again he surprised himself; he had never spoken so wisely, so tenderly, his words whipped about by the wind three stories up, the skyline dark with tombstonelike skyscrapers. For his bravery, he received a hug from this woman, who cried and let her body jerk against his, a sensation he took to bed and could describe as similar to a case of hiccups.

Poor woman, he remembered, looking at his knuckle where, eleven years before, a pearl of tear had fallen hot as wax. He was surprised her tear had not scalded his skin and left a hook-shaped scar, something endearing to fondle like a button. He recalled this memory almost every morning, his feet, in spite of his extra-thick socks, cold as the floor they rested on. He recalled this woman because she was the third woman he had ever hugged, the first being his mother, of course, and the second a *novia* in Mexico, both now gone from his life, possibly dead or so transformed by the rasping nature of time he wouldn't have recognized them.

Gus was a man living for that moment when he could retire and say to his feet, "You have done your job." He would then squeeze his legs, which he thought of as his own personal mules, and commend them as well. For their sake, he planned to sit on the patio for his remaining years, to watch TV or read the newspaper, to give his body luxurious soaks in the bathtub, despite the neighbor's radio, which vibrated through their shared wall. The radio was no more than a whisper, a nudge of sentimentality because the songs were all about love.

Stupid songs, Gus complained silently. But he was grateful the songs were in Spanish, not English, and that they were ballads or polkas, not that music called "rap." Occasionally the songs awakened in him a longing for his *novia*, some bird fluttering in the cage of his heart. When this occurred, he called up in his memory the woman on the roof and was seized with terror: love brings marriage and sorrow.

One morning his routine was broken. As a rule, he rose at six-fifteen and ate oatmeal and drank two cups of coffee, a habit that had puckered his mouth into deep lines. Then, if there was time, he tossed handfuls of seed to the pigeons that gathered on the small lawn of his duplex. But the clock had stopped sometime during the night. He rose at seven-twenty, too late to catch the seven forty-five bus at Fruitvale and be at work at eight-thirty, exactly fifteen minutes before he hoisted the flags in the bank's oil-splotched parking lot.

He turned over the clock radio, confused by the failure of the contraption to work faithfully, especially at this time in his career when he wanted to depart as an upright and noble employee. He rattled the clock radio and heard a noise, like a pebble in a tin can, but he was too rushed to bother with this thing that had let him down. He washed, dressed, and hurried out the door to catch the bus. Then he was forced to return to the apartment because he had forgotten his wallet.

"I'm late!" he muttered to himself as he slapped his back pockets in a sort of giddy-up gesture. In fact, he ran to catch his bus, a pound of keys jumping in his pocket.

But when he got to the bank with sheets of sweat under his uniform and ready to explain—no, apologize—his unusual tardiness, he was startled into a momentary standstill. He looked about the bank before his gaze floated upward toward the clock, which read 8:40, before his attention shifted to the general surroundings. There was a problem. No, the bank wasn't being robbed and no, a woman wasn't on the edge of the roof with her legs dangling like sausages. He was twenty minutes late—twenty-two according to the bank's clock—and no one seemed perturbed. Estela Rodriguez, the assistant manager, didn't look up from her papers, and John Sterling, the manager, busily tying his shoes, didn't shake a finger at him. The three tellers, two of whom were college students, were counting out bills, their eyes cast downward and lips moving as they registered the stacks of one-, five-, ten-, and twenty-dollar bills.

"But I'm late," he whispered, meaning not that he was formally late but that he had not arrived at the time he had always set for himself.

He took two slow steps, which he presumed would trigger an interest in his tardiness. He coughed. He jingled the keys in his pants pocket. Surely he deserved a reprimand, something to say that he had failed his position at least today.

The sweat chilled his body, especially in the flush of cool office air. It will come later, he told himself.

Aware of his first task, Gus turned on his heels and descended into the basement, where he brought out the flags of California and the United States, both of them heavy as laundry and, he noticed, in need of a wash. But it wasn't his place to mention this. His job was to raise the flags every morning and, after they were positioned in the sky, to open the bank's doors exactly at nine, no sooner, and take his place in front of the bank. From there he would occasionally spin inside to observe the surroundings with a beady-eyed scrutiny.

"But I was late," he muttered.

Gus carried the flags and, considering that he had jogged three blocks from the bus stop, did well to step lightly up the marble steps and into the lobby of the bank. He gazed about, still perplexed that no one had noticed his late arrival. At eleven minutes to nine, he stepped outside and first raised the U.S. flag, which started up limp as a coat on a hook. But as it rose higher, it came alive and snapped in the breeze that blew from the bay. He next raised the California flag and returned inside, where he waited with one hand on the door. At nine o'clock, he unlocked the door and held it open for the first customer, an absentminded fellow older than the building itself. This was Mr. Burnett, a widower in his nineties, who, on his demented days, wore his dentures upside down. And more than once he shuffled in with his pajama top underneath his coat, clip-clopping in slippers whose insides, once fur lined, were now oily and matted. The slippers disgusted Gus. To him, they resembled dead rats flattened nearly to nothing. But as with so many things, it wasn't Gus's place to say anything, just to open the door for such people, hoping that in time others would do the same for him.

"Gus!" Mr. Sterling shouted after Gus had led Mr. Burnett to the teller.

"Mr. Sterling?" Gus approached the manager, certain that the moment had arrived for two or three lashes of a reprimand. He almost longed for a moment of humiliation because if Mr. Sterling didn't care about lateness, then who would? And wouldn't that mean that his promptness all these years had been a waste?

"Gus, there's a man sleeping in the bushes," Mr. Sterling said, and hurried away without explaining.

But Gus knew. Occasionally sleepyheaded drunks or the homeless slept in the landscaping, slept in fits or recovered in the knife-glinting sun from the confusion of their hangovers. Gus turned and strode purposefully outside.

The figure wasn't asleep but slouching in a triangle-shaped flower bed at the corner of the bank. Gus could have easily turned on the sprinklers and let the man be washed into wakefulness. But buttoning the jacket of his uniform, a gesture that signaled business, he stomped toward the derelict, barking, "Get up! Let's go! This is no place to sleep."

The shaggy-headed man turned a milky eye on Gus, refusing to move. He was the color of oily rags.

"Let's go!" Gus whistled and clapped. He saw that the man was weak, a straw figure with clothes loose around his waist. His tongue appeared, wormlike, from the cavern of his mouth.

"*Estoy enfermo*, Gustavo," the man groaned.

"You're drunk!" Gus countered. Then Gus straightened up and studied this man, who lay back down, his stomach now a valley dappled with shadow. "How do you know my name?"

Gus waited for the man to respond.

"How do you know me?" he asked a second time. He considered kicking the man's shoe for an answer but held back.

The man sat up and slowly raised an uncapped Pepto-Bismol bottle from a twisted sack.

"*Mi estómago*, Gus." He ironed his stomach with the flat of his filthy hand.

Gus touched his chin and risked looking directly into the man's face, which was covered with dirt.

"Roberto?" Gus asked, head slowly shaking back and forth. "Roberto, is that you?"

Roberto's ragged appearance confirmed that work was more than an hourly wage, a week of vacation, a place to linger until one was old enough for retirement. Work was an embodiment of health. Raised in Mexico, Gus was familiar with work, from his first labor as a child in the fields and, later, as a teenager and an adult, in a shoe factory where he stamped out guitar-shaped soles on a machine. For Roberto to fall to such disgrace, right at the foot of his former employer's business . . . it was too shameful.

It also confirmed that the day had started off on a bad foot, all because of the clock radio, which Gus planned to slam against the back steps of his porch. He would punish it further by letting its wiry guts lie there for a few days before sweeping them up and tossing them unceremoniously into the garbage bin in the alley.

Gus grumbled. He admonished Roberto by saying that he brought a poor image to Latinos. Still, he squeezed the mouth of his plastic coin purse and out poured quarters, dimes, and nickels into Roberto's open hand. He sent him staggering up the street and advised him, "Get yourself together, hombre."

Having touched Roberto's dirty hand, withered arm, and sweat-soaked lower back, Gus washed his own mitts in the sprinkler, scrubbing them with a harsh back-and-forth motion. He examined his dripping hands, upset that what they had touched in raising Roberto to his feet was actually the past. He could do without that. He was looking toward the future, not the past, a future when he could sit in his living room with the colorful shadows of the television splashing over his face.

Other unusual occurrences that day put Gus on guard. A woman slipped in the tiled foyer and required an ambulance, which arrived like a scream and with a rack of pulsating red lights. Another customer spilled the complimentary coffee on herself, and two brothers waiting in line got into a fistfight.

"Boys! Boys!" Gus called as he separated the two, but not before he received a knock in the jaw himself. Later, he had a difficult time chewing his ham-and-cheese sandwich, his jaw milling slowly as he mashed his lunch to paste before he swallowed.

"You look like a camel," Julius the janitor joked.

"What?" said Gus carefully through his tender jaw.

"You're chewing like a camel, my man," Julius said. He churned his own jaw in imitation and, to Gus, did indeed resemble a camel.

Gus nodded and gave his coworker a bored smile when Julius began to provide a history lesson.

"Now, my people know camels." Julius sat down in a chair with its cotton guts spilling out. "Thousands and thousands of years of camels. We fled on camels, and camels gave us water because they got the humps, you see. That's how we get that water. We split 'em right away, like coconuts." He slapped his thighs and preached, "And your people—the Hispanics—they know donkeys 'cause I seen a lot of movies and not all of 'em are wrong." Julius further added that he was part Alabama Chickasaw and that made him and Gus, with his own Indian lineage, closer in blood than they realized. With that, Gus pretended to make out a commotion in the lobby and excused himself. No way did their bloodlines connect.

Suspicious of the day, Gus checked the sky for an eclipse or another sign that this Thursday at the end of the 1990s was unusual. He extended his palm outward, expecting rain, but felt only sunshine. He eyed birds and bearers of omens and took a step back when a cross-eyed man spat in the gutter. He shuddered when he opened a door for a woman whose chin was stiff with a spade of hair.

"Ay, *Dios mio*," he whispered. For a brief moment, he thought she might be a she-devil, not a customer with a horde of saved-up money. He crossed himself only after she passed.

The day became more bizarre when he returned home later than usual because he had missed his bus by seconds and was humiliated by blackish exhaust unraveling in his face. When he opened the front door of his tiny apartment, he encountered a small black-and-white dog with paws pressed together and head held high, a living portrait of a noble beast. The dog rolled his tongue over his mouth and barked once.

Gus slammed the door, confused, his heart jumping beneath

his uniform. He figured that he had opened the wrong door, maybe Mrs. Garcia's, the deaf widow and confirmed cat lover. Perhaps she was now taking in dogs; if so, he was going to complain to Mr. Harris, the ever-watchful landlord who lived three blocks away. One breed of animal—garbage-bin-hopping cats with their armada of fleas—was enough for this simple duplex. Why bring in dogs? he brooded. But the apartment was indeed his— a potted geranium picked up at a yard sale hung from the eaves just above his door. He was baffled; the day made no sense.

"My God," he mumbled, exorcising his confusion while sweat boiled in the wiry nests of his underarms. Why was this happening? Slowly he opened his front door again and peered in cautiously. The dog barked three times, far more than was necessary for Gus to slam the door and back away from his apartment of thirteen years, back away from his television, his bed and one dresser, his few portraits on the wall, his couch with the dent of his flat bottom. He backed away but stopped, rocking on his heels, hands trembling like brittle, rust-colored leaves. He was embarrassed that he, a security guard with his share of knocks, should be terrified by the presence of a black-and-white dog.

"Gustavo!" he scolded himself. "Surely you can confront this dog!"

But outside his job, he seldom confronted anyone or anything, living simply with no more than two forks to go with his two spoons. In fact, he was like Noah with an apartment for an ark. He was the proud owner of two straw place mats, two pillows, two Bibles (one in English and one Spanish, for he conjectured that God was partial to both languages), and two wicker-backed chairs, each routinely burdened with the weight of his working years.

He despised the unnecessarily complicated. Even when he bought the geranium, he didn't confront the seller, an Armenian woman who smelled of tobacco and hair oil, with good-humored

bartering. Instead he paid what she asked and carried away a geranium that had flourished on an occasional spurt of water from
an old Pepsi bottle.

Gus opened the door and stepped inside warily. The air was
stale as bread and—he sniffed twice—smelled faintly of bread.
The dog wasn't where it had stood just a minute before.

"Dog," he whispered, then louder, "dog!"

The dog barked from the kitchen, and its nails clicked against
the hypnotic flowery pattern of the linoleum floor. With a slice
of bread in its jaws, the dog trotted around the corner and a terrified
Gus begged, "Don't bite!"

He had reason for such fear. When he was nine, he and his
cousin Rafaela had played with a dog by dangerously flicking
matches at it. When they had run out of matches, they began to
strike the dog, their tiny fists outfitted in socks, the boxing gloves
of bored children on a rainy day. The blows were harmless as pelt-
ing rain, but when Rafaela pulled its tail, the dog snapped and
took a bite of Rafaela's ear, the lobe actually coming off like a
pinch of dough. The dog swallowed the pinkish flesh, and Rafaela,
five at the time and Gus's responsibility while the grown-ups were
working in the cornfield, howled with her hand to her ear and
her face raised to the full moon of her pain.

But that was long ago, in the twilight years of his childhood in
Mexico.

Gus could see that this dog was friendly, not a beast, that he
wasn't about to take a chunk from his ear. He asked, "What are
you doing here?" The dog's friendly tail whacked against a chair.
Gus had to push the dog down when it tried to raise its front paws
onto Gus's stomach. He slapped a paw and scolded, "Get down."

Gus noticed a hand-scrawled note on the kitchen table. He
raised it and nearly shoved it under his nose, his mouth puckered
as if he were drinking his morning coffee. The note was from
Guadalupe Contreras, a man who had first taken him in when

he arrived from Mexico nearly twenty years before, taken him in and taught him his first tidbits of English—"hello," "no, thank you," and "toast will be fine." The note said that he should take care of the dog, that its owner—his *novia*—had been deported by *la migra*, the border patrol. The dog needed a place to stay for a few weeks, possibly longer. Guadalupe knew where Gus hid a second key in the garden since he stayed with Gus when one of his three wives or dozen or so girlfriends tossed him out. He felt that he could enter as he pleased. And now he had left a dog to explore the bachelor's corral of meager living.

"Oh, Lupe!" he shrieked at the note written on Motel 6 stationery and in a script that implied haste. Gus let the note float back onto the table. He was distracted by the presence of the panting dog and, truth be told, that Lupe, age sixty-one, maybe older, was still fooling with women. He should be thinking of higher matters, Gus argued to himself and, stoop shouldered from his seven hours of standing on cement, struggled to strip off his jacket. But the weight and feel of the jacket stayed with him even after he hung it up in the hallway closet and sat on the couch, its springs groaning beneath him. When he took his shoes off his throbbing feet, a faint vinegary stench rose from his socks. But there was no rest. A moment later he was on the telephone, calling Lupe. He licked his lips for the moisture that it would take to scold his friend. He had no business unloading a dog on him, he steamed. But the telephone rang and rang. He hung up, sighed, and sat on the couch, studying the dog in silence. He speculated that the dog was old, perhaps older than he in dog years. He also saw that with its small, silky ears the dog might be a beagle, or a beagle and something else.

"*Cómo te llamas?*" he asked. Bending down, he reached for the dog's collar and rotated it until he felt a flat tag with Braille-like bumps. He felt the dog's breathing, moist as the steam that spouts from an iron. He squinted and read the tag.

"Flaco," Gus declared under his breath.

As he sat back into the couch, he considered leading the dog outside and quickly shutting the door on this unwelcome guest. He'll go away, he presumed. He'll just go away and live in an alley. Then Gus admonished himself as he envisioned the dog with his paws up on the side of a garbage bin. "You'll pay in hell if you do that," he heard himself say. And he felt it was true.

Still, when the dog licked Gus's face, he recoiled, with his hands coming up to protect himself from the rough tongue. There was no telling where that floppy organ had last unrolled, though he could smell the bread on its mouth. This much he knew.

Flaco brought a rear paw up to scratch his neck, his collar jingling. Gus saw the dog's penis smothered in fur.

"Put down your leg." He considered it pornographic that a dog should show his member to a complete stranger, especially if the stranger was him.

Gus always kept his apartment in order, things properly put away, from cups and glasses to the coat of his uniform, which now sagged in the hall closet, giving off the smells of this expired workday. Now fleas, the lowest of all insects, more loathsome in his opinion than the cockroach, were bedding down in his apartment. Gus scratched a leg, both arms, then back to his left leg, his frenzied imagination stirring with the possibility that he was being eaten alive.

"Lupe!" he scolded his friend, who, he pictured with certainty, was in the arms of a woman half his age. "*Sinvergüenza!* How could you do this to me!"

Gus rose from the couch to toss his socks in the bathroom hamper. There he washed his face, which sagged under his eyes. "This is me," he said absently to the mirror, whose glare was mean and brutally honest. He proceeded to his bedroom and opened a window, a breeze stirring the curtain to lazy motion. He eyed the broken clock radio, the contraption that had failed to wake him and thus set the day to a round of weird and unexpected events. He threatened, "I'll take care of you later."

In the kitchen, Gus found that Flaco had left teeth marks in a plastic bag of bread. He tossed the bread in the garbage, pleased that it hadn't been a new loaf but just a few slices. He thought of salvaging two or three of them, which appeared unscathed. But why take a chance? It was then that a knock thudded on the front door, a knock that he first attributed to wind. (He had noticed a pile of clouds when he rode the bus home, and the scent of rain perfumed the trees.)

The dog barked once.

Gus pressed a finger over his pursed mouth for the dog to be quiet, a gesture that simply made the dog march his front legs and wag his busy tail. When the thudding sounded again, his heart raced as he imagined *la migra*, the border patrol, on the trail of Lupe's girlfriend.

"Who is it?" His own words echoed back to him against the door. He recognized the voice as belonging to Mrs. Garcia, his neighbor, who was nearly deaf and possibly senile because none of her cats bore names, all of them referred to as "Kitty." "*Por favor*, don't bark," he warned Flaco loud enough for a person with good hearing to hear through the walls.

When he opened the door a few inches but wide enough to throw the light of his apartment onto their shared runway of a porch, Mrs. Garcia pushed her way into the doorway. She scolded him by saying firmly that dogs were not allowed in the duplex. Rules were rules, she insisted, not once but three times, each time louder than the first. In the early twilight behind her shoulder, her eyes sparked an intense volt of anger.

"But I don't know how he got here," Gus explained, palms out. He allowed her to butt him aside and take two giant steps into the living room. (Later, in bed that night, he would recall in horror that to his knowledge she was the first woman who'd entered his apartment. He thought it scandalous, he a bachelor and she a widow with a harem of cats.)

"What!" she yelled. The anger in her eyes increased in voltage, and her lower lip quivered.

"I don't know how the dog got here," he yelled for her benefit since her hearing was now closed like a fist.

She taunted him by saying that the dog probably had his own key. Her eyes lowered onto Flaco, who, at that indiscreet moment, kicked up a leg and began to lick his belly, pink as a starfish but soft as a water bottle.

Gus scolded Flaco to put his leg down, disgusted that the tip of his pink member peeked out. The pink suddenly extended like a finger, then was sucked back into the furry encasement. The dog stopped scratching to roll his tongue around his organ. Gus *had* to look away, hoping that Mrs. Garcia would do the same. But he could see from the corner of his eye that she was measuring the dog's appetite for his own private parts.

"Well?" Mrs. Garcia asked finally.

Gus couldn't begin to divulge his relationship with Lupe while the door was open. Rain had begun to fall, and wind slapped the leaves from the sycamore, rearranging autumn right before his eyes. His own anger percolated. He considered questioning her about her cats, one of which was seated on the porch, eyes red as coals.

Mrs. Garcia warned him that he had better get rid of the dog or risk hearing from Mr. Harris. She repeated this several times, as if trying to memorize her threat, and strode across the porch, cursing the rain. Gus returned to the kitchen with the dog meandering at his side. He rewashed his hands and, although he was no longer hungry, prepared his supper.

That night, he slurped his soup and ate two eggs without bread.

The bread, fetched from the garbage can and soaked in milk, had gone to this dog named Flaco.

In bed, he thrashed from belly to back and from back to belly in a sleep that was seven hours of epileptic fits. He woke tired, the morning gray as cement, and climbed out of bed to step into a disaster. He discovered in the kitchen a puddle of urine that, to his smallish eyes, was large as China, discovered this by first stepping into it with his left foot, already comfy in a clean sock, and then his right foot, also comfy in a sock.

"*Ay, Dios!*" he yelled. The dog had committed what he considered a sacrilege in his tidy kitchen. Surely any dog should know better, he insisted.

"Where are you?" he called furiously.

Flaco dashed boldly into the kitchen, panting as if he had returned from a prancing jog around the block. Gus wanted to slap the dog with the flat of his palm but instead stood quivering and breathing in gasps as if he, too, had pranced around the block.

For two days straight, his morning was ruined. He peeled off his socks, tiptoed to the back porch, and spread them on a wooden rail where he usually hung his underwear, thus away from view of those who might walk by and see such a rank display. He noticed Mrs. Garcia sweeping leaves from the cement patio; her back was turned to him. He noticed one of her cats on the fence, licking a paw.

Gus tiptoed back into his apartment.

"Why did you do this?" He stared at the lake of urine he had to jump over.

Flaco whined.

He washed his feet in the bathtub, holding up the cuffs of his pants, the water scalding hot as tears. He returned to the kitchen and soaked up the urine with a fistful of paper towels, for he couldn't stomach the notion of using a real towel. He loathed

146

the idea of someday bringing a once urine-soaked towel to his face.

He drank his coffee with both eyes stationed on Flaco and slowly rowed a spoon in his bowl of oatmeal. He thought darkly, blaming the clock radio for his turn of fate. If it had functioned, just as real time functioned, he would not have found himself in such a predicament. He understood that mechanical failures, clock radios included, slowed people so that their directives were altered. He had only to think of when city strikes occurred—last summer, for instance, garbage piled up, and the once direction-less flies knew where the feast lay in the stench of oven-warm garbage containers.

No, he wasn't superstitious, only a mildly religious man who occasionally mulled over the fate that had brought him from rural Mexico to Oakland, California. Still, if that clock radio had functioned, he would have risen at six-fifteen yesterday and none of this would have happened. His eyes floated up to the clock above the back door: 7:03. He had sufficient time to take Flaco out.

Outside, Flaco sniffed the small lawn of the duplex. Gus watched that Flaco didn't migrate into Mrs. Garcia's petunias. The flowers were far past their prime, but she would consider it a breach of neighborly conduct if she should find a single dog's paw print among the drooping heads of her flowers.

The dog sniffed the grass in a dozen or more places, his black nose flaring, before he finally lowered his fur-skirted bottom inches from the grass. Gus had to look away when Flaco nosed his own droppings.

"I could never be a dog," he said to himself. He waited for the steam of this morning mess to dissipate before he took a rip of newspaper to take away the evidence. "*Asco,*" he moaned as his fingers absently moved over the soft, pliable, and still hot dropping. He quickly disposed of it in the garbage bin in the alley, a mistake because as he was departing, he encountered his former

147

neighbor Billy, though Billy joked he preferred "hillbilly." The man was proud of his ignorance and his appearance—whiskers pale as straw and the roving eyes of an idiot trying to lock onto something meaningful. Back then—and now, Gus noted—he kept a knife on his belt and occasionally took it out and stabbed the lawn, his anger building up with each thrust. He stabbed the lawn and screamed the names of numerous presidents, though his true complaint was against a Laundromat that once turned his whole wash pink. He said he would have been a different person if he hadn't had to wear pink socks.

My luck, Gus fumed. This person, this hillbilly, was wearisome. Gus could have lived with Billy stabbing the ground, but he couldn't stomach his odd jokes. He recalled how one morning as Gus sat in sunlight on the rickety porch punched with termites, sat with the textbook *Step Forward with English*, Billy rushed out of his apartment, shirtless, and hollered for Gus to come in, quick, because something was on television that he, no, the whole world, should see. Billy spread out his arms and commenced to make swooping circles, each repetition speeding up until his arms were blurry as propellers. At the time, Gus could say only a few words in English, one being "okay." But when Gus ventured forth suspiciously into the apartment, his own eyes floating up and about in imitation of Billy's roving stares, he discovered that the TV on the kitchen table was not on. Billy was giggling, almost snorting, with a hand on the refrigerator handle. For a brief moment Gus thought Billy was going to throw open the door and show himself what he had stolen from Safeway. But Billy only stomped the linoleum floor with his scuffed engineer boots. The floor stomping produced finger-long cockroaches that raced from under the refrigerator, their bodies ticking against one another. At first, Gus couldn't assemble in his mind what he was seeing—a jigsaw puzzle falling from the table? A handful of pinto beans hurled to the floor? A jar of nails breaking? When he realized they were roaches, Gus held his heart, as if to calm this pulsating organ, and jumped back, screamed. He ran out of the apartment, leaving Billy laughing with his mouth open, revealing the broken-down fence of his teeth.

That was years ago, and now Billy was standing in the alley with a stick and a cardboard box. The fence of his teeth had completely collapsed. Still, Billy smiled and shook Gus's hands, saying how much he missed him and those days on Harper Street. Billy admired Flaco and ran his hand through his fur, gently at first before he gripped the fur on the back of Flaco's neck and almost lifted the dog, Flaco's front paws coming off the ground.

"Dogs like that," Billy said when Gus, suddenly furious, pushed his hand away. "They like to be picked up. It's good for their circulation."

"It's good for no one, hillbilly!" Gus yelled, not amused.

Billy grinned brightly that Gus remembered his name. He tapped the box with his stick and asked, "You wanna buy some oranges?"

Gus couldn't believe this riffraff. Right in Gus's presence he had handled Flaco roughly, and now he was peddling oranges stolen from the neighbors' trees. Gus turned and whistled to Flaco, and together they hurried into his yard. He was careful to latch the gate, which Billy tried to wiggle open. He called, "Come on, Gus. I was just playing. I wouldn't sell you no oranges." Gus stood in the yard where he could make out Billy behind the slats of their (thank God) tall fence. Then the sky rained two oranges that thudded on the lawn with a dull percussion and didn't roll very far. "Your English got real good," Billy called out. Flaco sniffed the oranges, but Gus left them there.

America is turning ugly, he told himself. And he told Flaco the same when he bent down to pet him.

In the apartment, Gus put down a layer of newspaper in the bathroom, understanding fully that because Flaco was a dog, thus a shade or two below man, he couldn't control his bowels. The dog's instinct of propriety was not—and never would be!—developed. "I'll be back after a while," he said as if the dog could understand. He snapped off the light and ruffled the dog's fur, cooing a tender, "There, there." He closed the door behind Flaco, who didn't whine or bark. Guilt or no guilt, Gus had to get to work.

Gus was thrilled when he caught an earlier bus, one that was nearly empty of sour-faced commuters making their way to work. He arrived at the bank twenty-three minutes early, a record he hadn't attempted, but one bestowed upon him by the unexpected arrival of the bus. The ornate roll-up gate, installed to keep the homeless from sleeping near the heating vents, was raised halfway. Gus raised it further, locking it in position. One duty was done for the day.

After he disarmed the alarm with two keys, he let himself in. He was surprised by how dingy the bank was without the overhead lights. He spied the coffee machine, cold but dark with day-old coffee. The sugar cubes lay scattered like dice. He wanted another cup of coffee, but it wasn't his job to make it. This belonged to Martha, a bejeweled teller who threw off an aura of perfume every time she strutted past. He launched a sugar cube into his mouth, a rush that sweetened the morning that had started out rudely but was beginning to smooth out in his favor.

He was proceeding into the basement lightly when he caught sight of Mr. Sterling, his wide back turned and arms wrapped around his waist. Gus wondered how he could contort his arms like that, wrap them around and actually move them. The arms were desperately reaching for his bottom, as if he were fiddling with his underwear. Then he saw Mr. Sterling push Mrs. Rodriguez aside, her mouth blotched with a candylike smear, the kind of smear nasty children acquire from eating greedily.

Gus could feel his eyes widen and remain wide when he set his legs in motion down the steps. He kept one hand on the rail because he was nearly overcome with dizziness from this immoral exhibition. Confounded at what he had witnessed, especially with Mrs. Rodriguez's groping hands on Mr. Sterling's bottom, Gus sat in the basement, his post when not guarding the bank. He brooded with his head bowed, twisting the ring on his finger clockwise. Mr. Sterling? he thought. Mrs. Rodriguez? He knew both were married, each with a framed portrait of their families set on the altar of their paper-strewn desks. He pictured the two naked on the floor, next to the cardboard stand where customers picked up information on home and car loans. He pictured Martha, the teller, applauding their middle-aged screwing and the college students hovering above, also clapping to the rhythm of their sex. He even saw old man Burnett bend over the writhing bodies. Gus admonished himself for such a thought. Was something wrong with him?

He stood up, rifled through his locker, and collected his hand-cuffs and wooden baton, the weight of objects he knew well. This morning, they seemed like appendages when he attached them to his belt. His mind was not right. He banged his locker shut, sat back down, and worked the heels of his palms into his closed eyes.

"What's wrong, man?" Julius asked as he came into their room. A spray bottle of window cleaner was hooked on his belt and a blue rag hung like a tail from his back pocket.

Gus gazed up at Julius, then lowered his face.

"Look at this, Gus." Julius held up a soiled dollar bill, torn in half. "Martha threw it in the garbage, said it was no good. And I said, 'Girl, give it to me. I know suckers in the world I can fool.' And that includes my ol' lady." He laughed at that, his open mouth allowing Gus a terrible view of spoiled teeth.

Gus squeezed his eyes shut, hoping that a flood of tears might wash away the memory of the two adulterers.

"And don't it look like George Washington's smilin'," Julius remarked. He chewed the inside of his cheek, the meat of a thinking janitor. "Heard that his teeth were made out of cherry wood. Lucky a woodpecker didn't drill holes in 'em."

Gus didn't respond. He turned quickly to the clock over their lockers and saw that it was eight forty-nine. He was nearly five minutes late!

"*Híjole!*" He pushed himself out of his chair. He fumbled for the flags and jogged upstairs, a heavy assembly of keys spanking his thigh. He slowed before he appeared in the main area of the bank, embarrassed for both Mr. Sterling and Mrs. Rodriguez. Perhaps he was more embarrassed than they were for themselves.

"I'm fifty-nine," he said absently. He didn't know what he meant by saying that. He repeated it at the top of the stairs and a third time as he paraded out, blinking because the lights were on and humming almost imperceptibly.

In less than ten minutes, when he personally unlocked the double doors of the bank, the day would officially start and the mysterious, almost confessionlike transactions would repeat themselves over and over until four in the afternoon. In his own life, it took Gus a thoughtful five minutes to write out a single check, his lips moving dryly as he wrote the date, the amount, and finally his signature, which closed everything like a handshake. His own bank was near his apartment; he feared the tellers, especially Martha, knowing how little money he had accumulated during his lifetime. He was aware that some considered him as insignificant ("our little ol' guard," he once heard, and "shorty" at another time). For them to rifle through his personal finances would have been too much to bear. So he kept his money at the American Savings and Loan near his apartment.

Nevertheless, he took pride in people who knew about banking matters, all executed electronically on fibers as thin as his own thinning hair. He swallowed. He strode into the customer area with the flags, now positioned respectfully in his arms, and turned his head only slightly toward Mrs. Rodriguez's desk. She was seated there, her mouth now once again a red pucker of lipstick. She was on the telephone, head tilted so she didn't need either hand to answer the caller. Her hands instead were busy as crabs on the top of her desk, possibly searching for a contract, a bankbook, an 800 number, something urgent because the hands were scuttling. When she looked up in his direction, he snapped his head away and marched across the room to do his duty of raising the flags. He was, after all, five minutes late and counting.

Outside, Gus reveled in the cool bay breeze, tainted almost imperceptibly with the smell of metalworks from the factories situated near the bay. He paused for a moment and pinched the flags between his thighs and reached for a handkerchief in his breast pocket. He splotched sweat from his brow, blew his nose, and patted his sweaty brow again.

"You're fifty-nine," a voice said.

Gus was confused. Was that *himself* saying that? Was he throwing his voice or going crazy?

"You're retiring soon," the voice added.

When Gus wheeled around, he saw that the voice belonged to Mr. Sterling.

"Mr. Sterling?" He felt short as a penguin against the tall, much younger boss. His entire body was, in fact, swamped by Mr. Sterling's shadow, which blotted the ground.

"The man's back in the bush," said Sterling in a husky voice that revealed a recent cigarette, the residue of bluish smoke momentarily escaping from his mouth. "Let's get rid of him—*pronto!*" Mr. Sterling winced at the flags between his legs. "Gus, that's no way to treat our flags. You can do better."

Only after Mr. Sterling departed did Gus peer at the flags between his thighs. He hoisted the flags from that preposterous position into his arms and hugged them as he walked lamely toward the flagpoles. You are so foolish, he reflected angrily on himself. He raised the flags into the breeze, slapped his hands free of the grime from the chain, and ventured to attend to the person in the flower bed.

"What are you doing there?" Gus shouted. He saw right away that it was Roberto, his face gray as ash and his mouth a dark, wet hole. He wanted to escape, knowing full well that it was more complicated than just shooing Roberto away. He stopped with his pants cuffs flapping about his ankles, and after a hesitant moment proceeded toward Roberto in a sort of funeral march. "What are you doing back here?" he asked, this time concerned.

Roberto touched his stomach.

"You're sick because you're filthy." Immediately Gus regretted his cruelty. He growled at himself and raised his face toward the sky, where a blimp was seemingly stalled over the faraway Oakland Coliseum. A football game—the Raiders versus the Kansas City Chiefs—would be played there on Sunday. Already the blimp was making its silent rounds over the Bay Area.

Roberto sat up and mumbled, "Gustavo, help me."

"Help you!" Gustavo snapped. He remembered how Roberto had thrown the jacket of his uniform at him and skipped away arm in arm with a drunk sidekick. "You laughed at work, and now look at you, hombre."

Roberto didn't answer. He swiveled his head away and when he turned it back slowly, Gus saw that there were tears in Roberto's eyes.

"*Compa*," he moaned.

"You call me *compa*?" Gus asked. He could now make out the faint motor of the blimp, but he didn't bother to marvel at its passing. His attention was locked on this . . . bum. There was no other word for a disheveled man who had fallen without grace into the flower bed of his former employer.

His sneer slowly relaxed into the simple pucker of an old man. "Roberto," he pleaded with his face and his arms. "I only have two weeks." He pleaded to Roberto that he was near retirement and desired to depart with dignity, not to mention a monthly pension and perhaps one or two gifts, remembrances he could touch daily and that would make him reflect with pride, "Ah, yes, I did my duty." He wanted nothing more than to sit in the backyard, even if it was populated with Mrs. Garcia's numerous kitties. But to sit there, half in shade and half in sunlight, to permit his bones to find a new position within his flesh—that would be meaningful and worth the years of pacing on cement, of putting up with snide janitors like Julius.

"Let me stay with you," Roberto asked.

Gus couldn't believe what he was hearing: this sickly apparition, someone he hardly remembered, asking for a bed in his own apartment! First the dog Flaco, and now this man with a hole in his stomach!

"*Imposible!*" Gus shouted.

Roberto touched his chest and lowered his face, the clanging of the chain against the flagpole like a hammer on an anvil. After a brief moment, he pointed a dirty hand in the direction of the bank: Mr. Sterling was gesturing at his watch, glinting in the sunlight like a knife.

Gus moaned and patted his thigh, where the keys jingled like coins. For the first time in nineteen years, he had failed to open the bank as was prescribed in the verbal contract between the bank manager of yesteryear and himself, abruptly a relic of yesteryear as well.

"*Compa,*" Roberto, now staggering to his feet, called from the flower bed.

Gus withdrew from Roberto, a poisonous lowlife, and hurriedly approached Mr. Sterling. But before he could bow before him with a stuttering excuse, bow for a reprimand that would shrink him even further in his baggy uniform, Mr. Sterling swirled around and reentered the bank, where once again the mysterious transactions of money began. His boss didn't have words for an aging security guard with no sense of time.

On the surface, the morning was as eventless as a yawn, though Gus worried about his failure of duty as well as about Roberto, who wobbled away with smoke-colored leaves pressed to the seat of his pants. But this sick acquaintance returned an hour later and paraded in front of the bank. To Gus's shock, Roberto even attempted to spy inside the Brinks armored car when it arrived at ten thirty-six. Gus had to hold him back and babble to the guards whose thighs were saddled with real guns that this lowly figure was nothing but a street person. They had nothing to fear, Gus tried to laugh, elbowing Roberto in the ribs.

"They got a heck of a lot of money," Roberto told Gus, who finally pulled him away from the armored car. Behind a pillar, Gus lashed him with threats, which Roberto took with a sunken chest, a lowered gaze, and a shuffling of his feet. He was hurt.

Gus then skipped to catch up with the Brinks guards. It was customary that he usher them into the bank, a charade that usually made him proud for his close proximity to great amounts of money. But this morning, he was a few steps late. The guards had to wait at a swinging door, which Gus buzzed open by feeling under the counter for the not-so-concealed button. He watched the real guards with real guns march toward the safe before he returned to his post outside the entrance.

Later, when Gus was called to move a broken calculator into the basement, Roberto invaded the bank for a cup of coffee, his grimy, rootlike fingers gnarled around the sugar cubes. Gus found him exploiting these freebies when he returned from the simple moving task. His hair, limp as it was, nearly jumped on his scalp.

"GO! *Vaya!*" Gus shouted as he strode toward Roberto and glanced nervously about, certain that he was at fault for not keeping such vagrants from its environs. Mr. Sterling observed from behind his desk and Mrs. Rodriguez stopped her conversation on the telephone. Gus hissed, "Come on, let's go—YOU."

"But we're friends, Gus," Roberto managed to argue as he chomped on a sugar cube.

Gus's cheeks burned. He yanked Roberto away from the coffee, led him through the double doors, and deposited him onto the sidewalk, where he scolded him. Gus returned to examine the sugar cubes for specks of dirt. He tossed a few suspicious ones and with a water-dipped napkin wiped the handle of the coffee machine, for germs could easily lurk there, moist and warm for hours, and possibly make a customer ill.

Roberto drifted up and down the street, where he occasionally begged with an outstretched palm mapped with misfortune and rivers of black sludge. He held out a hand for spare change, but the passersby did just that: passed by without a momentary regard for his plight. Gus witnessed Roberto's pathetic begging and clicked his tongue. Frequently he passed his time observing cars and passersby, his attention falling on them long enough to assemble an opinion, no matter how insignificant. Although voiceless at work, a mere shadow that lengthened on the walls of the Walnut Bank, he would divert his mind from boredom with such mental chatter as, "That car has a bad muffler," "That young lady's dress is too short," or "That man is certainly wearing a toupee." Thus he kept busy as he stood or paced in front of the bank, occasionally touching his baton when a suspicious vagrant circled the block more than twice. But today was another kind of circus. His attention was fastened on Roberto, who appeared and disappeared, staggered, and crawled in one instance when he tripped on the sidewalk.

"The shame!" Gus howled at the plants in the canopied entrance of the bank. "The man must be drunk!"

Toward two o'clock, after much nail-chewing worry for both

himself and Roberto, he finally relented to Roberto's request. After all, he was a Christian at heart, and wasn't it true that Guadalupe Contreras had allowed him to stay at his apartment when he first arrived from Mexico? Gus recovered this remote history in his conscience. Who could say that he was stingy and without concern for a fellow Latino? He chewed a thumbnail to a bloody wound in discovering this, his own tenderness.

When Roberto next swung past, more pathetic because he was drinking from a milk carton likely scavenged from a trash bin, Gus mumbled, "I give up," waved him over, and gave him the address to his apartment. He also gave him two dollars for the bus as well as instructions to wait on the porch. As an afterthought, he warned him that if Mrs. Garcia was in the yard and grumbling about dogs, he should ignore her, just tell her that he was a friend, nothing more.

"*Compa*," Roberto said, shivering. A pearl-shaped drop of milk clung to his chin.

"Don't call me *compa*," Gus reprimanded. This word, he felt, should be employed only between brotherly men. "And wipe your mouth, hombre."

"Gustavo," he cried. "You're a friend for life."

Gus swallowed this statement like a bitter pill.

"Can you do something for me?" Roberto asked.

Gus sighed, as if to ask, what now?

Roberto asked if Gus could to stop at the Salvation Army or a Goodwill and buy him a shirt and a pair of pants, socks and a T-shirt. He added to this list a sweater, shivering with his arms crossed over his chest to draw attention to his apparent fever.

Already he's costing me, Gus calculated.

Roberto stumbled away, studying the address written on the back of the deposit slip. He crossed the street and vanished, though his unfortunate smell lingered in Gus's nostrils until the bank closed at 4:00 P.M. By then, Gus was exhausted from worry.

Gus took a bus packed with people, all of them tired as mules, some smelling of mules. But instead of his regular stop on Foothill, he got off on litter-strewn East 14th. He was glad to step into fresh air and away from a bus ride that had turned into a sauna where the riders' moist breathing was stirred about by crying babies. He crossed the pocked street and hesitated in front of a Goodwill store that was large as a barn. He hated such places, frequented by— he cursed himself but couldn't help thinking it—the poor. With a deep breath, he budged open the glass door, greasy with finger-prints. He was overwhelmed by the exhaust of stale air that is-sued from the dozen lazy-eyed customers as well as the piles and racks of merchandise. He maintained a stance for a moment, siz-ing up the apparel and motley kitchen gadgets.

During his first few years from Mexico, he bought used clothes at such places. He bought khakis and work shirts, and he sourly remembered socks and boxers, too. He remembered purchasing a white disco suit for Guadalupe Contreras's wedding to a woman from Yugoslavia. Guadalupe laughed that neither spoke English well and that their marriage would work out attractively, each of them tongue-tied and incommunicable as mutes. The marriage lasted less than a year, and, for a resilient Guadalupe, the pain disappeared like a bruise. He was married again within months.

In menswear, Gus held up a pair of jeans, scrutinizing the ta-pering length of the legs. A pumpkin-colored paint stain stood out near the front pocket. He tossed them back and picked up another pair, then still another, all of them flawed with stringy holes, rips, bleach stains, or faded patches at the knees—for work-ers who crawled for their living? He finally settled on a decent pair and next chose a blue sweater with an emblem of a sailboat, although he calculated it possibly too handsome for Roberto. He rifled through a pile of cheaply made T-shirts, most of them soiled, slack around the collar, or emblazoned with sports logos Gus knew almost nothing about. Instead he gloated over a plaid cowboy shirt with imitation pearl snaps, a bargain at a dollar-fifty. Roberto is three inches taller than me, he estimated. With this in mind, he pressed the shirt up to his own body for a loose measurement. It seemed perfect. He lodged these clothes under his arm and was preparing to see about socks when a girl stopped him. She was clutching a sweater in both hands when she asked if he could help her.

Gus blinked at her, confused.

"It's about my mother," the girl whispered, then sighed and dropped her voice. "She wanted me to have . . ." The girl hesitated, sighed a second time, and turned away with her gaze lowering to the floor.

This elfin girl left abruptly. Ordinarily Gus would not have bothered to inquire of others who could only half explain themselves, but he saw that her eyes were red, and wasn't that a sprinkle of tears clinging to the side of her nose? Watching her slow and painful steps, he considered whether to sidle next to her because he feared that she might faint. After his nearly two decades as a security guard, he had witnessed his share of customers—usually men suffering from diabetes, heart conditions, or just plain drunk—faint in midstep.

"Do something," he heard himself say, but his feet didn't move. She was now by the formless mountain of bras and girdles and other mysterious feminine gadgets. Since he was timid about such intimate articles, he waited until she wandered toward the slacks hanging on a circular rack. He approached her, where he feigned a scholarly interest in the slacks on hangers, a stupid pretense for getting close to her. She knows I'm here, he thought. His fingers danced absently past one pair of slacks, then others. And then they spoke.

She recounted how her mother had died and that her father had taken all her clothes—boxes upon boxes and armfuls of dresses he waltzed to her car—and given them away to this Goodwill.

She had found one sweater here. She held it out; the sweater was a white angora with four slightly yellowed buttons. It was the only item of clothing she had found, but she knew there were others, perhaps in bins or boxes or on the racks or still in the back room where clothes were sorted. She had asked the cashier, who bitterly explained that it would take too long to hunt out these specific articles, and besides the workers in the back, all lazy souls, could barely help themselves, let alone customers.

Gus was confounded by this openhearted confession, then ravaged with sorrow as she recounted for him how her mother had died of cancer, but had lived eight months longer than her father or doctors foresaw. She died in a recliner, she said, and there was sunlight on her shoulder, which made her passing beautiful. (I don't want to hear no more, Gus thought as he took a step backward, warding off the details of such a confession. He scolded himself—Be a man!) Then, biting her lip, the girl stopped, a shudder moving her shoulders. She ran a finger under her nose, and her eyes filled. Behind her a puddle of late afternoon sunlight shimmered on the floor. In a few minutes, its warmth would slip across the floor and disappear in the late afternoon.

"But you work here, don't you?" she asked. She scrutinized the patch on his uniform, which said simply, Security.

Gus said no, that he didn't work there, but surprised himself as he offered to help her search the store. He said this in spite of the frightening intuition that maybe all these clothes—mounds of jeans, the mismatched shoes with flopping soles, the tangled sweaters, and the faded and worthless shirts—belonged to people who had died. He shuddered and became momentarily apprehensive as he imagined the outcome of his own death—God forbid, not too soon after his retirement, please—when his clothes would be sorted, boxed, and hauled to such a place, where they would be mauled by bargain hunters such as himself. Uneasily he squirmed with the used clothes under his arms.

The girl smiled at Gus, a miracle in itself. How long had it been since a young girl had smiled at him? How long since someone outside of work asked for help? If he had been more softhearted, he would have felt tears soak his eyes and slowly blur his already poor vision. He would have shaded his brow with one hand while the other raked away tears. Instead he turned slightly and his hands blindly smoothed a pair of orange slacks. He couldn't believe this about himself, he a security guard—weathered by sun, rain, and the worst elements in rude people—ready to sob inside a Goodwill store? Who would have expected it?

"But you wouldn't know my mom's clothes," she countered. She touched his arm, a second miracle because a girl had never touched him, except for an occasional bump on a rocking bus plunging down Broadway. He felt limp. He could have thrown himself into the bin of T-shirts and not all the clothes there could have soaked up his sorrow for this young girl. He pictured her mother, dead in a recliner, and the sunlight pulling away to be slowly replaced by a rising tide of afternoon shade.

How could he locate her mother's skirts and coats? He leaned against a bin of clothes. His attention fell on his shoes, scuffed but polished, worn at the heels, and thin as his own human hide. Would he have recognized them if they were piled among the holocaust of other shoes?

The girl excused herself for bothering him.

"No, I bothered you," he stammered.

She apologized as she stepped backward. "I'm sorry, but I thought you were security for this place."

What could he do but let her turn and depart? He clutched Roberto's new wardrobe under his arms. A rock lodged in his throat, and his tongue—heavy as a dead lizard—was unable to spit out a single word. He made his purchases in silence and hurried out of the Goodwill store, wiping his eyes. For a long time he would remember the girl's profile, the thumping in her throat, her smile, her mother's death in sunlight—details absorbed like aspirin, but which brought no relief to his pain.

He walked down East 14th, and when he heard a dog bark from the back of a trunk, he found himself running.

Roberto was not waiting on the front steps of the porch. Gus called for his wayward friend, who didn't materialize by staggering on his gimpy legs, those getaway sticks reduced to bone and little flesh. In some ways, Gus was relieved because his life was already set, and what did he need from a sick person? Suddenly he confronted a hot anger slowly stoking alive inside him. His face darkened. He seethed that Roberto couldn't follow one simple direction. "*Ay, Dios,*" he growled to the geranium hanging above his door, unlocked the front door, swollen with autumn's first rain, and entered, anticipating a deluge of dog urine soaking the carpet. Except for a single fly chewing up the silence, there was no commotion. Then a single bark disturbed the quiet.

Gus tossed the bag of secondhand clothes onto the couch. He opened the bathroom door, letting out Flaco, who, with tail wagging mightily, raised up his front paws and churned the air until he was standing upright against Gus's pants. Holding his front paws, Gus danced him toward the living room. He patted and frisked Flaco's dense fur, a friendship that was surprisingly warm. The dog licked Gus's throat, salted from the long day.

When Gus saw Flaco's muddy paw prints on the toilet seat, he immediately guided him outside, where the dog pressed his nose to the lawn, sniffed the earthy perfumes of dirt and spiky grass, and searched out a place. He sniffed the grass and lifted a leg against a scraggly rosebush, his steamy liquid springing forth like a burst pipe. God forbid that Mrs. Garcia should come bickering loudly, Gus prayed as he glimpsed two of her cats on the porch, both sleepy-eyed in a fluttering patch of sunlight. If she did come from her apartment, he would argue that cats and dogs were almost the same breed—notice the fur, the four legs, the tails, the whiskers, and the marauding fleas within their glorious coats. Sure, one offered a bark and the other a meow, but both slept during the day and, if permitted, would prowl the night. Gus was equipped for an argument, but her door remained closed.

Relieved, Flaco commenced to trot away, slowly at first but soon under the power of a quick gait that propelled him halfway down the street. Gus called for him to stop, but the dog added speed to his trot, his short, aged legs scissoring their way across one lawn and the next, halfway up porches, down porches, over bicycles tossed on lawns, and through piles of raked leaves, their sunlit edges rattling in the wind. *"Ven acá!"* Gus called as adrenaline rushed into his veins and his lungs burned as he tried to keep up with Flaco, who zigzagged under parked cars and trucks and dangerously close to speeding vehicles. Gus now saw one difference between cat and dog: the canine, once on a mischievous scent, was hard to follow.

He chased the dog while—in his mind—he had become a buffoon as he jogged knock-kneed, shouting ludicrously, "Flaco, Flaco!" He was prepared to give up when the dog abruptly stopped, sniffed the debris in a gutter, and carefully lowered his bottom. An out-of-breath Gus observed this beastly spectacle, particularly nervous that a neighbor in this rough area might yell at him and the dog. "Oh, Flaco," he muttered. Gus felt it was him making this private act public. Yes, it was him lowering his bottom shamelessly in the gutter choked with leaves and littered with potato chip bags and candy wrappers, the contributions of teenagers. He begged Flaco to please hurry, but the dog, grimacing like a human, took his time as he produced a rope of excrement. Gus forced himself to look skyward, his interest directed high above to the Goodyear blimp hovering between wafers of transparent clouds. As before, it was silent and ominous; in the early dusk, a panel of lights read Go Raiders, followed by Go 49ers.

164

"Sports," he grunted at the wishy-washy blimp.

Afterward, with a hand fitted under Flaco's collar and stooped over like an old man, he steered the wandering dog back to the apartment.

An exhausted Gus threw himself onto the couch, undisturbed by the sweat that seeped from his face and neck, yet another bath of salty excretions. He permitted Flaco to explore the apartment and poke his nose into this and that, for he was too tired to bother with him. His gaze fell on his hands, peppered with age marks. He remarked to himself that his legs did all the work, pillars for his body, but it was his hands that appeared old and foreign. If, by chance, they had appeared in a photograph in a glossy magazine, he wouldn't have recognized them. No, he would have argued, those aren't mine. They belong to some field-worker, a janitor, a liver-damaged drunk sitting out his last days in a rest home. He flopped them from his pinkish palms to the rough backs, astonished by how old they had gotten. And he hadn't even noticed.

The shadows of dusk absorbed the colors of the living room and would soon swallow the splattering of sunlight on the wall. He wondered if he had enough strength to open a can of pork and beans and set its contents on a burner. He thirsted for a drink of water, but his shoes were heavy and his legs juiceless.

Gus heard Roberto's muffled voice, then silence before he made out the voice again, chuckling and louder, sounding insane if you didn't know the man. He perked up, weasel-like, scrutinizing his small living room where he sat and the dining room where his vision reached. He heard Roberto's voice once more, this time making out the word *sandía*, "watermelon" in Spanish. Puzzled, he got up and tiptoed into the hallway, freezing when Roberto's voice reached him from somewhere. As he opened the hall closet, he expected Roberto to fall out like an ironing board. But he stared only at his two winter coats, saturated with the weight of rained-on years, and the octopuslike vacuum cleaner with armfuls of extensions. There was an old broom chewed to stiff bristles from use. He gripped the broom and whispered, "Junk." He placed it out on the front porch.

In the kitchen, Flaco sat on the floor, panting, a princely picture of comfort. Gus became still when Roberto's voice echoed again. He grew scared as he realized that he didn't know him, really, and that maybe he had become, who knows, crazy from living on the street. With his eyebrows knitted, he stared at the ceiling, where perhaps Roberto lurked in the small crawl space. Impossible, he figured, and why climb up there—for what? He scanned the kitchen, but there was nowhere to hide. Even if Roberto was insane, he was too tall to fit in the cupboards next to the peanut butter, the popcorn, the dented cans of half-priced soup, and his favorite Quaker Oats oatmeal.

"Where are you?" he called, ready for an ambush. "Where are you . . . *compa?*" The faucet dripped, ticking in the sink against his breakfast bowl.

Flaco rose to his feet, sidled up to Gus, and sniffed his hands before proceeding to lick them for salt and tenderness. Gus laughed at this tickling and gently spanked Flaco's fur. "I'm hearing voices," he told Flaco, who smooched his face when Gus bent down to one knee. "I taste good, huh?"

Flaco smooched his neck again, which made Gus giggle and push the dog away. Gus decided to take a shower. In his bedroom, he got out clean underwear and snapped an angry look at the clock radio, formerly lit with the time but now solemnly dark.

In the shower, while curls of steam rose to his thighs, Gus lathered his head until it was a turban of pinkish suds that stung his eyes shut, which was okay by him because he had already seen far too much of the day. He hurt himself purposely with hot water and punished himself further by turning on the cold water, a yin-yang of self-abuse. "You're such a child, old man." He laughed at himself when he shut off the water, stepped out of the shower, and began to floss his body dry with a thin towel. It was then he again made out Roberto's voice vibrating from inside the dead space of the wall. But which wall? He listened while beads of water slid from his oil-less body.

"This is not right," he shouted in English, then Spanish, as he toweled off, stepped into his underwear, dressed quickly, and began to search his apartment. This has to stop, he growled in his mind. Only when he opened the front door did he detect Roberto's voice coming from Mrs. Garcia's apartment. He couldn't imagine how he had charmed himself onto her premises, how this riffraff from the street could befriend a deaf woman with a platoon of kittens. It didn't measure up.

"Ay, Chihuahua!" He made his way across the porch and knocked on her apartment door. His fist thundered like a hammer. When the door swung open, flooding the porch with yellow light, a washed-and-combed Roberto was holding a slice of sandía, the smile of this out-of-season watermelon gone.

"Gustavo!" Roberto crowed. "I've been waiting!"

Gus's anger warmed his head, which was still wet from the shower. His thin hair was matted to his scalp. A single drop of water hung like an earring from his earlobe.

"Is it raining?" Roberto asked, actually taking a step onto the porch and peering out at the dark. "Funny, I didn't hear it start raining."

Gus could have taken that watermelon and rubbed it into Roberto's face, but he saw that this previously soiled derelict was clean. His body, more starved than Gus had imagined earlier, his arms and legs hoe thin, was dressed in fresh but out-of-date clothes. His shirt buttons were in the wrong holes. He asked Roberto why he hadn't waited on the porch as he had been told. Roberto had a quick answer: he had waited, except a most marvelous thing occurred. Mrs. Garcia called him to help to change a burned-out lightbulb. In truth, there were six lightbulbs, maracas he played

167

for the kittens who scrambled at his feet. And *la Señora* made him climb onto a chair and bring down a box from high in her bedroom closet, retrieve a rubber ball from behind the refrigerator, plus read a letter from social security. Roberto had to read the letter three times to make sense of its contents.

As Roberto began to describe his last six hours of service, rewarded by an expensive watermelon from Lucky's, Mrs. Garcia shuffled up and stood next to Roberto before she volunteered, "I love dogs, but I like cats better. You have a nice dog, Gustavo."

The two were an unlikely pairing—one a homebody and the other a street person whose days were governed by sunset and sunrise. She smiled with a kitten in her arms, a single seed from the watermelon pasted near her mouth. She told him to please come in, joking that with the door open, the flies were escaping. Her grin resembled the smile of Roberto's toothless slice of watermelon.

Roberto pulled Gus inside and immediately bragged about his shirts and pants, the sleeveless T-shirt, the shoes parked near the muted television—clothes that once belonged to Mrs. Garcia's husband, long dead, but now were his because Mrs. Garcia knew the meaning of pity. With that piece of information, Gus wanted to guide himself out of her apartment and back into his hovel. He didn't want to hear this business about dead people's clothes, especially ones mothballed and augured with years of dust.

At the dining table, Mrs. Garcia raised a meat cleaver and, with momentum that could cut through a burly neck, sliced a rugged piece of watermelon for Gus. She brought him a butchered slice and prodded him—all the while again raving that she liked dogs—to please sit down on her couch, which he did, in the process waking two mother cats. They raised their small triangle-shaped heads and showed only mild interest in Gus before returning to their slumber.

Roberto giggled. He recounted that while he was fetching a key from the floor furnace, he learned from Mrs. Garcia that their families were from the same town of Progreso, Texas. They hugged at this piece of news and named names of people they knew from that dusty border town—the Trejos, the Garzas, the tightfisted Acostas, the unfortunate Baptist family that burned to death in a house, the Silvas, burned but not forgotten because a football scholarship was created in their honor. Mrs. Garcia even went as far as confiding to Roberto that she had almost married his uncle Alberto and would have except he was already married. Besides, that conniving Alberto didn't last very long. One Easter morning he was kicked by a donkey, its iron-clad hoof giving him first a headache and finally lockjaw a week later—a nail had punctured his forehead like a staple. This was all retold in a rush of words as Gus sat on the couch, gripping his watermelon. He searched for a way out.

It arrived when he heard Flaco bark. He rose and announced, "I must feed my dog." Out of politeness, he took three rapid bites out of the watermelon, smiled, and handed his unfinished portion to Roberto, saying, "Take this." He then poked Roberto's stomach. "Seems like you're feeling pretty good."

Roberto patted his stomach, now slightly pushed out with two or three meals, and remarked, "I was just hungry." He turned to Mrs. Garcia and yelled, "HUNGRY!"

With the trumpet of the word *hungry*, Mrs. Garcia shuffled to the kitchen and yanked open the refrigerator, her face lighting up from the twenty-watt bulb as she searched for leftovers to feed Roberto, once a derelict but now a prince in a deaf woman's house.

Gus warned Roberto not to be too long, but said nothing about the buttons on his shirt.

That night Gus rolled in a fitful sleep, aware of Flaco pacing the apartment and Roberto snoring on the living-room floor. But he didn't shake Roberto awake and demand that he be quiet. He didn't have the heart to lock Flaco in the bathroom or tie him up on the front porch, where he might have barked, howled, or simply set his large head on his paws to wait for the first pink rubbings of dawn to sprinkle light over the trees. No, Gus rolled in bed and got up to lower the toilet lid when Flaco began to drink from the bowl. In the bathroom, moonlight lit up the chrome-plated faucet and the edges of the mirror with just enough light for him to see that Flaco's wagging tail was something like love. He ruffled Flaco's fur and cursed his friend Guadalupe Contreras, but then, as an afterthought, thanked his old *compadre*, because now with a dog such as Flaco he might—he swallowed a feeling caught in his throat—talk to another warm creature, even if this creature could only bark. With a painful lower back, head thumping from a headache, and feet throbbing, Gus returned to his bed with its rack of thin mattresses. He returned with the smell of Flaco's fur on his hands.

Before too long, Gus felt what he first appraised as a lizard on his shoulders. He was startled even further when he discovered that the lizard, now close to his throat, was actually a hand. It was Roberto, who moaned, "*Compa*, I think I ate too much. My stomach hurts." Gus sat up, took a deep breath, and sighed. "Ay, Roberto, you're so much trouble." He regretted his words and showed his true feelings by making his friend a cup of *yerba buena* tea.

As they sat at the dining table, Roberto slurped his tea and volunteered that he had been living in a garage for the last two months, not a bad place because there was a window, a nice bed, and a blackberry vine that had crawled stubbornly through a crack in the wall. Roberto lectured that the blackberries were loaded with vitamin C plus a cancer-fighting agent whose name escaped him. He stood up and raised his hands over his head. He tiptoed and stretched his arms toward the ceiling, crowing that the vine was taller than he, but so packed with vitamins that its berries could heal people—or so he had read in a magazine he found right there in the garage! Gus yawned from the flogging of such detail. Roberto added that you had to watch your head because the ceiling was low in one place, like a coffin lid. He parted his hair and forced Gus to feel the lumps on his scalp. "See! Can you feel 'em? Like walnuts, no?"

At dawn, Gus rose exhausted with his small eyes made even smaller from the puffiness of a poor sleep. He studied Roberto's shape on the floor and draped him with an army surplus blanket. He rocked his shoulder and quipped that Roberto's snoring was waking the birds. But Roberto just ground his teeth and let out a cavernous moan. Gus allowed him to sleep. He washed, dressed, and shuffled to the kitchen, where he made his oatmeal and ate at the kitchen table. He was relieved to know that in two weeks he would be allowed to sit forever—in the patio, at the park, and occasionally in a back pew in St. Elizabeth's. A chill struck him, though, because the word *forever* was a lie: he would lie longer in the confines of a grave than sit or stand. He slurped his oatmeal for warmth.

He let Flaco out for his morning round but begged the dog to hurry for fear that Roberto might rouse himself to bring up yet more recollections of blackberries and vitamins. He was simpler than Gus remembered, this Roberto from Progreso, a Texas town that admittedly he had never heard of.

Luckily Flaco urgently lowered his bottom, rejoicing with a bark when he finished depositing a monstrous mound. He examined his accomplishment with a probing nose. Gus shoveled up the mess, thankful that his puffy eyes didn't permit him to see more than was necessary. He ushered Flaco into the apartment and wrote a brief note for Roberto telling him to help himself to eggs and tortillas or oatmeal if he was an oatmeal eater.

Gus reluctantly locked Flaco in the bathroom with a spread of newspapers and left with a jingle of keys, music for the early morning. He rode a bus packed with commuters whose faces were furious and brutal because every day offered the same routine.

171

They worked because they had to eat, Gus surmised of these angry workers. For the rest of the ride, he turned his attention to his hands, trembling from the bus's vibration on the street. They seemed to leap on his lap at every turn.

When he arrived at the bank, Gus noticed that the ornate iron gate was pulled up and locked in position and the plants were wet, as if it had rained. Fat, Buddha-shaped drops clung to the leaves and soaked the ground richly dark. He became cautious when he saw the entrance was open, not locked. He leaned a shoulder into the glass door, which gave easily under the pressure of his weight. Something is wrong, Gus thought, seriously wrong, because as he quietly entered the lobby his nostrils, always sensitive—even at his age—pulled in the smell of coffee. He first assumed that Martha had arrived early, but when he sniffed the air, he could not pick up the trace of her perfume.

Gus advanced a few short steps, then paused while his heart galloped under the heat of his jacket. He pivoted as he scanned the familiar surroundings. He noticed a human smell that surprisingly arose from himself of all people. The smell born of fear rose in an invisible smoldering from his hair, under his clean shirt, and down where it counted, from his crotch. His tongue became dry as a dead mouse. He called, "Hello," but the greeting seemed to drop like ash at his shoes. He was suddenly ashamed of himself, he a security guard at the same bank for all these years. A great, big hand should come out of the sky, he thought, and slap me a good one.

A moment later Gus staggered back on his heels when a man, dressed in a uniform not unlike his own but filled to the hilt with muscle, appeared at the top of the basement stairs. A chill rose from Gus's ribs, gathered strength, and moved across his chest and settled on his shoulders. This stranger, who appeared to have eaten rocks for breakfast, not watery oatmeal, stared for a long minute before scissoring his short but strong legs in Gus's direction. Gus touched the place on his belt where his baton customarily rested, but he felt nothing.

"Who are you?" the man inquired as he approached from across the lobby.

This set Gus off. A question of this sort had no place in these surroundings, where he single-handedly defended—along with the eyeballing cameras, for sure—the deposits of so many customers.

This man is no one, Gus thought. He sucked in a chestful of air until the jacket appeared to fill.

"Who are *you?*" Gus groped boldly, though right away he felt that perhaps he was too callous. He could have placed more feeling on *are* or the owlish *who*, but it was too late to recall the accusing *you*. He longed for Mr. Sterling to rescue him with an explanation, or even Mrs. Rodriguez with her bloodred fingernails. But this was hoping for too much.

The man marched in clean, echoing steps across the polished floor and stopped within a foot of Gus, a draft from his arrival actually moving across Gus's face. The man was bald, except for hair around his temples and the back of his head, which rested on a pad of muscle. He stood with his legs shot out, a stance that might suggest to an onlooker that he was ready to throw powerful blows. His eyes were flat, and his tongue rolled over his teeth, swabbing them of something—the paste of a doughnut or a bagel, or possibly one of the rocks he devoured that morning? The man informed Gus in a heavy accent, "I'm security guard. My name is Roman Khrushchov."

Gus's jacket deflated like a balloon. He turned halfway around, then cast his eyes on the floor where he belonged—defeated and bloodied by the inevitable. Yes, you heard right, Gus told himself. This bald fellow with more muscle than two men, and with a heroic first name to top it off, is your replacement. He wished for a hand from the sky to not only slap him but also choke him within seconds of his death. But of course, nothing of the sort happened. Gus only breathed in more of the brewed coffee and made out the sounds of a car door slamming in the street, a shopping cart of a homeless person rumbling on the sidewalk, and a dog barking far away. No, Gus didn't have the presence of mind to play out a mental game, as he might have on a boring day, that the dog's bark might possibly belong to Flaco. He could only think of this new person, his replacement, and how his time was up. He heard Roman Khrushchov's soldierly steps recede.

"Wait for me!" Gus scrambled after Roman, who was descending the stairs into the basement, their territory, the place where they "hung," as Julius put it. Gus hankered to ask why the front door was open and did so only after Roman brought out a bundle of keys to open the washroom.

"Yours no good," Roman informed Gus in a flat voice.

Gus let this sink into his head—water seeping through rock. How could they be no good? he wondered. His hand, a gopher, crawled inside his pocket and brought out his keys. He jingled them at his friend.

"Yes, these keys," Roman said. "Locks are changed." He offered no explanation but turned abruptly to the cabinet for the flags—the United States flag was placed respectfully on top of the California flag.

"No, it's too early," Gus yelled when he saw Roman retrieve them gruffly, his pudgy fingers gripping them with more strength than was necessary as the blood rushed from his fingernails. Gus decided that the man was a brute and his English was too poor to assume his duty as security guard with any dignity. "We don't do the flags until eight forty-five."

Roman narrowed his eyes at Gus.

"Why?" he asked.

Why? Gus asked as he recoiled from such a question. You, a new employee, a rent-a-cop for all I know, a man who has not guarded a single minute in front of the bank, asking me "why?" Who are you, anyway? Whereas I have stood and paced in one place longer than any other guard in Oakland, in rain and harsh sunlight, in acid smoke during the hills fire of 1993, in a barrage of hail that knocked off my eyeglasses, too. Gus steamed. He told him that it was customary to raise the flags at exactly eight forty-five, to which Roman replied, "Times change."

Gus swallowed.

"For today you can do what you want," Roman commented.

Let's show some respect, fellow, Gus told Roman, almost adding the word *comrade* because Gus, an astute observer of immigrants, knew that Roman was from somewhere like Russia or one of those Balkan states, a foreigner who was quite different from an immigrant like himself. He was from Mexico! Gus bravely grabbed the flags from him and hugged them, desperate that the first task of the day was nearly behind him, something precious that would soon be a part of the past.

Gus hurried from the basement, leaping the steps three at a time, and stopped only when Mrs. Rodriguez, already at her desk and on the telephone, wiggled her fingers at him. He wasn't sure if the wiggle was for him to come over or go away. Gus cut a glance at the clock: it was eight thirty-four, nine minutes early, but considering that Roman Khrushchov was behind him, he hastened out of the bank and into the parking lot.

After the heat of this frightening encounter, the cool air refreshed Gus's body and even forced him to sneeze from a chill. He thought of wiping his brow, but he could hear Roman's footsteps behind him. So he made it to the flagpole and was fishing for his keys when Roman's voice boomed, "They don't work no more."

Roman used his keys to unlock the padlocked chain and raise the flags in vigorous yanks. Gus stood, like an anemic fish with pulsating gills, watching the flags flutter and snap as they reached tree level and higher. Gus considered saluting, for wasn't this the last morning he would stand in this place, below the two honored flags he had raised so many times? But he wouldn't embarrass himself as long as this nasty brute stood next to him. He wouldn't understand the kind of respect that flags deserve, he a foreigner who should work harder, Gus thought, at dissolving his heavy accent.

Gus strutted angrily away, and when he pushed the bank door, he discovered that it was locked. The glass fogged with the heat of his breath, which slowly cleared to reveal Mrs. Rodriguez scraping something off her high heel, scraping in such a way that she resembled a bull hammering a hoof against the ground. He had to wait for Roman to let them back in. When he did, he marched over to Mrs. Rodriguez, now seated behind her desk, and asked for an explanation.

"No, we have not hired an extra security guard," Mrs. Rodriguez said brightly. "It's your lucky day, Gus."

Gus knitted his brows.

"It's your last day," she announced with a spread of her arms tinkling a jamboree of bracelets. She stood up and, to his astonishment, pushed her hand in his direction, this woman who never cared what he thought. He recalled how once at the copy machine when she had passed gas in his presence, she didn't redden with embarrassment but simply wiggled the back of her dress to release the smell. She continued rolling a breath mint in her mouth, as if this disgraceful folly was something like a sneeze or a cough. He remembered that clearly—April 12, 1993—because he had to help jump-start a customer's car and hurt his lower back in the process. He returned rubbing his lower back and shivering, with a chandelier of raindrops hanging from his hat. Later he caught a cold, but did he stay home in bed? No, the next day, he positioned himself in front of the bank because it was honorable to work even if you were sick and even if you had a hundred days of sick leave.

"This is my last . . . day?" His eyes slowly fell onto her calendar, which he could not read from where he stood.

"But we have cake!" Mrs. Rodriguez chirped, her tongue venturing out of her mouth and licking her lips. She went as far as rubbing her stomach and adding that it was chocolate cake from Heavenly Delights, a pastry shop, where you couldn't go wrong. When Gus refused to smile, only squiggled his mouth, she tapped her watch and reminded Gus that it was almost time.

Gus turned and noticed that it was three minutes to nine and that Roman Khrushchov was nowhere in sight. He turned back to Mrs. Rodriguez and snapped, "Yes, but my keys don't work!"

She didn't flinch. She only asked if he had met the new security guard and, after looking left, then right, bent her head toward him and in a conspiratorial fashion whispered, "He's not really hired, like you were, but rented, you know?" He could smell the coolness of breath mint on her tongue, that and coffee.

The word *were* struck him like a blow, and a second blow landed when he began to decipher the meaning of *rented* and its opposite— *sold*. It seized him that for these nineteen years he had been sold property, which made him furious because he was certain, yes, positive, that, in spite of his dwindling stature in his floppy uniform, he could never be sold. But he recovered quickly from this mental anguish when he spotted Roman moving briskly across the lobby and toward the door. While he wheeled around and studied Roman's progress, Mrs. Rodriguez explained to Gus that he had accrued so much vacation time, in addition to sick leave, that the bank decided to let him go earlier so he could enjoy his retirement sooner, especially now that it was fall. She mentioned his pension, plus a small bonus, but Gus didn't hear any of it. Instead he watched Roman open the door a minute too early. Gus shouted, "It's not time!" to which Mrs. Rodriguez scolded him that he shouldn't yell, then joked that if he wasn't a good boy, he wouldn't get a bite of his own cake. He snarled at her, pivoted, and rushed over to the door, but it was too late. Mr. Burnett, with his dentures upside down and still in his slippers, entered with his three bankbooks tied with rubber bands. His voice boomed, "Is it daylight savings time?"

"What?" Roman asked, his hands propped on his hips.

"I eat lunch at one o'clock," Mr. Burnett stated through dentures that were clapping loose. "I eat lunch at one when it's daylight savings time. Dinner I skip."

Gus pulled on Roman's arm, intending to explain in private about Mr. Burnett, but he might as well have tried pulling the bank off its foundation. Gus couldn't budge this muscle man.

"He's a special customer," Gus whispered, then added slightly louder, "You opened up too early."

Roman didn't respond. He stomped outside the door and yelled for two boys on bicycles to get the hell away. One boy dropped a potato chip bag before he languidly pedaled off, so slowly that to Gus, it seemed the wobbly bike might lose its inertia and topple over. Just like the boy himself, in life.

Gus returned to Mrs. Rodriguez, who was already busy on the telephone with two lines blinking. She shook her head at him. He insisted that he talk to her, but she said, "Gus, this is important!" She sweetened her tone, though, and told him to come back in a few minutes.

A few minutes, he muttered silently. He left and got his baton and handcuffs, ignoring Roman when he asked what the old customer meant by daylight savings time. He ignored him because he wasn't sure, either.

So this is how it's done, Gus mused. The task of breaking the news about his early retirement was given to a woman who passes a thunderclap of gas and ignores it and, worse, who is capable of fondling a man not her husband but her superior—and at eight-twenty in the morning and nearly under the portrait of the bank's founder! He realized a grabby person such as Mrs. Rodriguez, an adulterer with only a chocolate cake on her mind, was the one to send him away quietly. Mr. Sterling had taken the day off. Gus pictured him fiddling with his ass at the ninth hole of a deep-green golf course.

Gus took his place outside the bank that morning and only left when the Brinks armored car arrived at ten-thirty. Roman tried to snoop inside the idling carrier, but one of the guards asked what the hell he was doing in a rough tone that pleased Gus. Gus didn't bother to introduce Roman Whatever-his-last-name-was. He led the guards into the bank and wanted dearly to tell them— David he knew better than the younger man named Patrick— that it was his last day. But he held back this piece of information; after all, he was a professional—a word that he didn't find embarrassing in the least when describing his position—and what mattered was that the six bags of money were delivered.

Afterward Gus paced outside the bank, and when Roman paced in his direction, Gus spun away, his head high, for he was in a dark mood. He had nothing to say to this person, who struck him as rude, no, a voyeur, when he caught Roman openmouthed and eyeballing a young woman as she entered the bank. Gus could have scoured Roman's eyes with Comet cleanser; this was no way to greet a customer, admittedly pretty but with probably only a meager amount of money invested in the Walnut Bank.

"Animal!" Gus cried when he heard him growl after the woman passed. Turning away, he walked toward the flower bed, where he expected Roberto to be lying with a daisy in his hand and his stomach perhaps now less of a valley. He stared at that space where yesterday, just short of twenty-four hours ago, he realized, that vagabond from the past lay starving and filthy beyond recognition. He bent over and picked up a few candy wrappers and oily potato chip bags.

Gus assumed his position outside the bank with his back not quite against the wall, thus his weight resting firmly on his legs, his mules, he called them. No, he was going to stand like a man, a *mexicano*, right to the end of this final day as an employee of the bank. He would bake in the full sun of the morning. In the afternoon, he would say nothing of the wind that moved in with angular shadows cast from buildings and that caused him many earaches. No, he was not going to allow this new security guard, nine steps to the left of him, to see him falter once. If only a would-be bank robber appeared, he would really demonstrate all that he had learned during his employment. If only another woman would scamper to the top of the building and shout, "I'm going to kill myself. Save me, Gus!" He would know what to do, he a veteran of such emotional skirmishes.

But his mind became twisted with dark ruminations when his eyes drilled hatred at the fancy bagel shop across the street. Young people—late risers, college students, the fortunate who lived in the Oakland hills—were raising coffee cups to their mouths when others, such as himself, were hard at work. He knew their kind, white kids who grew up to be white adults, all of them fortunate to be suited up in the kind of skin that would eventually allow them to get better jobs.

His anger built up speed, not unlike a train, and all of a sud-den he was cursing the entire state of California, followed by Texas and New Mexico, where he had had bad experiences, and finally the entire United States, everyone fortunate except him. He had to stand watching young people waste money—and time!—eating and drinking, no, worse, he had to stand right next to a Russian who was, at that instant, picking what could only be an ugly substance from his hideous nose. He hated Mexico, the state of Monterrey where he was born, raised, and stamped out soles for shoes! His anger built up until his eyes caught sight of the flags whipping in the wind. At that moment he sensed a ghastly error. The flags were on the wrong poles: the United

States flag should be on the right pole and the California flag on the left pole.

"Look what you have done!" he snapped at Roman, whose own small but flint-sharp eyes were set on a man near the flower bed.

Roman turned his head and jerked his chin at Gus, as if to ask, "What?"

"The flags are all wrong!" He vented his anger by saying that only a fool would raise the flags on the wrong poles and if he couldn't get that right, then how could he take care of other, far more urgent, matters?

"Like what?" Roman asked.

LIKE WHAT? If Gus had been stronger or at least a few years younger, he might have slapped the fellow, squeezed him into a headlock, and forced him to denounce his despicable Russian motherland. Didn't he have any pride? They were hired not only to oversee loads and loads of money but also, in the course of their presence, to be human symbols for children, feeble retirees, those in wheelchairs, many others, who, if molested in the street, could turn to them and shout, "Help me!" He would have carried himself into a frenzy, but Roman stepped away from the wall, now hot with sunlight, and put his wheeling legs into action as he propelled himself over to the flower bed, where a man dressed in loud clothes was on all fours. Roman poked a finger at this person and yelled, "Get the hell away!"

Gus squinted as he raised a hand to his brow in a sort of salute. "*Ay!*" Gus yelped.

Gus sprinted to the flower bed, where Roman harangued Roberto to leave; he punished him further by slandering him with, "Lowlife bum who ruins the country!" Roman's fists were both closed as he belittled, from all appearances, a man down on his luck. This threat forced Robert to rise on his bony knees from a graveyard of dying or dead flowers.

Gus told Roman not to insult his friend. Roberto nodded to Gus's friendly tiding.

"This is man you know?" Roman asked, and spat a miraculous glop, the kind of liquid that might spurt from a run-over frog. "You know this bum?" He told Gus how he had seen him plenty of times before at his last job as a security guard at Lucky's. "Always begging! Always begging! In Poland, we cannot tolerate such behavior."

Ah, Poland, Gus thought. He apologized to Russia for his error. Then he absorbed a deeper truth: This man worked at Lucky's? This man prowled the aisles, looking for thieves who snagged cough syrup, candy, and Bic lighters? And now he dares to guard a bank with millions of dollars at stake? He would have spat, but he found that sort of behavior unacceptable, even if Roman was insulting Roberto, dressed in the cowboy shirt he had bought him yesterday at Goodwill. The snaps of his shirt, thank God, were fastened right.

Roberto argued that it wasn't true, that sometimes his ragged plight opened up wallets and purses without his asking. He blurted, "I'm looking for my crucifix." He was certain that he had dropped it there yesterday, and Roman asked what he was doing there in the first place. He accused him of urinating in public.

"Hold on! This is my business," Gus stated, not knowing fully what he meant. But he repeated it and plucked a dried petal from the sleeve of Roberto's shirt. He praised Roberto by commenting on the good fit of his new shirt, to which Roberto said how much he liked the snaps.

Roman sneered at the two of them, spat, and walked away, hiking up his pants. After Roman was some distance away, Gus heralded to Roberto—and to passersby if they cared to listen—that it was his last day, that they had changed the locks, that this brute was his replacement, that Mr. Sterling intentionally skipped work, that he would be served chocolate cake—grief spouted to a friend, who himself had been let go four years before. He cried that he should have stayed in Mexico, where he would have worked until there was nothing left of his body. That way he wouldn't be much bother when they buried him in just a length of muslin cloth and a few boards to shelter his poor flesh.

Roberto squeezed Gus's shoulder and told his friend that he was talking nonsense. Gus could only nod, then stoke alive his anger.

The two searched for the crucifix, which Roberto described as one of his few personal possessions. It was silver on wood and in his death agony Jesus's head was tilted to the left, though Roberto had seen some crucifixes where his head was tilted to the right. Roberto said that it depended on which country the religious articles were cast. He said the same thing about his feet — the right foot was, as a rule, nailed over the left foot, but occasionally the left foot was nailed over the right. It all depended upon the country, Roberto preached as both his left and right hands scratched at the earth.

As soon as they found it, Martha the teller came into the parking lot, hollering, "Gustavo! Gustavo!" For a moment, Gus imagined the bank was besieged by robbers with their faces hidden in ski masks and toting guns huge as car mufflers. He slapped the dirt from his knees and jogged toward Martha with Roberto in tow. But when he was within a few feet of her, he saw that she was smiling. Her glass earrings were alight with a fiery sunlight.

"It's time for your cake!" she sang, and clapped, a blossom of perfume floating about him. She hooked her arm onto his and pulled him, her strength bewilderingly strong for someone who simply licked her thumb and counted out twenty-dollar bills all day. Taller than he, especially with her hairdo balancing on her head, she hauled him into the bank. Roberto followed, fitting the crucifix around his neck.

Mrs. Rodriguez was standing before a cake flat as a tract house, salmon colored with a white awning of frosting all around and with seventeen candles burning at different heights. He didn't count the candles at first but instead eyed the onlookers eyeing him. They were all bank employees except an elderly couple who happened to be making a transaction at the time and recognized a freebie when they saw one. They only had to linger by fooling with the brochures on home and car loans.

"It's pretty nice looking." Roberto glowed. He punched one of the balloons tied to the table and laughed.

When Gus saw Mrs. Rodriguez frown at Roberto, he confirmed that he was a friend by squeezing his arm. He almost started to say that he had once worked here, but he held his tongue for fear that he might start yelling. Yelling what, he didn't know, but if she had said something against Roberto, such as that his clothes were old or that his milky left eye was impossible to view during chitchat, it would burst something inside him and his legs, his mules, might kick over this cake set on a wobbly card table. But she was mum regarding Roberto's presence. She just frowned until her attention once again fell onto the cake that would ruin every-one's appetite for lunch. He noticed that it was eleven twenty-seven.

One of the tellers gripped the table with both hands as Gus, a good soldier but filled with something like hate, was handed a knife and asked to cut slices for everyone. Why am I doing this? he asked himself as he balanced his anger and the heavy blade in his hand. Why do I have to act this out? he wondered before he counted the candles that didn't add up to his years of service, two short if the candles were indeed his years burning to smoke and a black wick. He cut a second piece for Mrs. Rodriguez, who begged for a flower this time, and cut two manly pieces for Julius, who had come up from the basement to say in a deep voice, "Gus, you done yo' job. You done it good." He cut slices for the linger-ing customers and then for another who happened to come in with a boisterous complaint but whose voice sweetened after two bites from a piece that was almost entirely frosting and yellow flower. Gus chose not to raise a stink about the two missing candles, those missing years that added up to more heartbeats than this bank had money. They wouldn't even understand, he lamented, except wisecracking Julius, who was suddenly somber and whose face, like the candles, was melting from something he would know very soon.

Gus played with his cake, smiled, heaved a small bit into his mouth, and said to his coworkers, who were dispersing because the bank was filling with customers, "It tastes just like I expected."

Gus was released after an order of pepperoni pizza arrived and everyone snatched a slice when time allowed. Gus protested that it was only twelve-seventeen and that he had to work until four in the afternoon. But Mrs. Rodriguez, now in charge, chuckled that he was silly, that this was his special day, that he would receive his first pension check in six weeks, and that he shouldn't take anything that didn't belong to him as her gaze cut icily to his baton and handcuffs.

"I'm sorry, Gus," she immediately apologized. She allowed her mouth to pout like a clown's to further show how ashamed she was for suggesting that he might leave with something that was not his. "That was poorly put. But look at what we have!"

Martha's perfumed hand held out a small, brightly colored present. Gus accepted it and considered rattling it but simply fit it into his pocket. He placed it there, though Mrs. Rodriguez and Martha stomped their feet and demanded that he open it right then. Oh, come on, Martha repeated, but Gus told them he would open it later. He had had enough of them, was in fact angry for his dismissal when he still had time. In Spanish, he whispered to Roberto, who was scraping cheese from the pizza box, to wait outside.

His face pinched with undefined hurt, he trudged downstairs to place his baton and handcuffs, plus the small badge that said Gus, on the table. He thrust his hand into his pocket and brought out the useless keys. He unhooked his wide, leather belt, bank property from years before, and let it hang over the back of a chair. No one would accuse him of stealing. He nearly sobbed, "But they took my years," except he felt a birdlike grip on his shoulder.

It was Julius, who said in Spanish, "*Cuidado, amigo.* You take care, now. I be joining you one day." He chewed the inside of his cheek thoughtfully. "Our people suffer. And like I say earlier, I part Chickasaw and you be some kind of Indian from Mexico. I can tell, amigo. You got the sadness right here." Julius tapped his heart with a fist.

Gus squeezed Julius's shoulder and assured his janitor friend that he would take care of himself. He said this while studying Julius's face. He thought, Maybe Julius is Indian, and imagined him with a headdress and his painted face before a bright fire. But instead of a spear, he pictured him with a broom.

Gus's plan was to dash out before Mrs. Rodriguez or Martha could say good-bye or try to hug him or even before he had to accept the good-bye card the tellers had all signed for him. He sneaked up from the basement and at the top of the stairs peered around the bank, flush with new customers because it was Friday, the busiest day of the week, when wallets and purses were filled, only to be emptied by Sunday. He made up his mind he would not play along. And he wouldn't let Roman, positioned outside with his back set firmly against the wall, lock his eyes onto his own. He didn't want his last memory to be of a man greeting his departure. Instead, once Mrs. Rodriguez and Martha's backs were turned, he walked briskly across the lobby and out the door. "*Oyé.*" He whistled to Roberto, who was tying his shoes, once Mr. Garcia's but now his. "Let's go, hombre." They dashed across the parking lot and crossed the street. Only after walking a half block did Gus glance back. He snarled, "The flags are on the wrong poles."

Roberto squinted in the late sun and remarked, "I knew something was wrong."

Gus and Roberto walked for a few blocks before boarding a bus from downtown Oakland to the Fruitvale area. They drifted toward Sanborn Park, where wobbly drunks leaned on the play structures. They had sat there for only twenty minutes, basking like spiders in the sun, before a needle-thin female junkie came up and asked Gus, "You the police?"

Gus gazed down at his uniform, then up at the gap-toothed woman. He shook his head no.

They left the park and walked toward Cesar Chavez Library and would have entered except it didn't open until two. Through a high window, a light shone and someone was singing in Spanish. From there, they walked three blocks and sat in front of the abandoned Living Spirit of Almighty God Church, whose windows were smashed and where fat-throated pigeons now warbled. Roberto repeatedly told Gus that that bank was no good and that their interest rates—3.7 percent for a standard passbook—were lousy.

"I'd give my money away before I let them have it." Roberto stated this firmly by a shake of his head and the pounding of his fist against his thigh.

Gus didn't reply because he was certain that Roberto had no money. He also didn't say anything when Roberto continued by saying that if he had a million dollars, the lousy bank wouldn't get that amount, either. But when the sum went up to twelve million dollars, Gus said he needed to be alone. Roberto tried to lead Gus into a conversation about clothes, thanking him over and over for the plaid shirt. He crowed about the shoes and the suit jacket that once belonged to Mr. Garcia—whoever he was or wherever he was, heaven or hell—but now were proudly his attire. Gus repeated that he needed to be alone, though he was tempted to tell Roberto about the girl he had met at the Goodwill store.

Roberto kicked a pebble at his feet, sighed until his chest deflated under his new used clothes, and accepted the apartment key that Gus pressed into his palm.

"Take Flaco for a walk," Gus said.

"Yeah, a walk," Roberto said dreamily. He rose and shook out his pants legs. "I like to walk dogs."

Gus watched his friend, his *compa*, clop away in shoes that didn't fit. He watched until he was a mere specter blending among other specters carrying packages and groceries, carrying their own Roberto, how he must have suffered on the streets those years. He pondered Mrs. Garcia and her platoon of kittens. These two people seemed real, their shadows far more solid than the walls of the bank. He then tried to remember the name of the bank manager who first hired him nineteen years before. He could see his face, but his name escaped him no matter how hard he squinted his eyes shut and retraced his past. But that man doesn't matter, he found himself saying to his legs, those mules that kept him upright in any kind of weather. He reached into his pocket for the present and stripped off his jacket. He left both the present and the jacket there and walked toward the library, which was now open.

Gus wandered into this place where parents and children revolved like molecules from books to magazines to the copy machine to the glowing screen of a computer. It was quiet, yet not quiet, busy with shuffling feet and books opening and slamming closed. A telephone rang, a water fountain gurgled, and some whiskery gentleman snored in a faraway corner where sunlight fell.

Gus brought out his eyeglasses and, leaning over a rack of newspapers, some in English and others in Spanish, he culled through the front-page news. He read the ghastly headlines of famine and wars, of a bus driven off a mountain curve in Peru. With the news all terrible, he wandered into the children's area, which held a large carpet for children to sit on and read. He touched the books on the squeaky revolving stands, touched them and then was touched himself. He looked down. A child, no, a baby only few months out of his diapers, Gus figured, was pulling on his pants leg and asking to be lifted. The child pitched his arms up, smiled, begged to be raised. Gus was confused by this child, who had now mounted his shoes and was riding them as Gus took a step, then another with no one saying anything. The unlikely couple danced until Gus was smiling and suddenly was laughing as he lifted the baby—*híjole*, he weighed so much—into his arms.

Gus rose on Sunday to the sight of a blimp. He parted the curtains and surveyed the shadow of the blimp raking across the ground where his tomatoes and chilies grew through the cool summers of Oakland. He peeked skyward but turned when Flaco barked at his closed door.

"*Ay*, Flaco," Gus scolded when Flaco raised his paws on the door and scratched to be let in. He remembered then it was daylight savings time, an hour added to his life, and he fell back onto his bed, longing suddenly for the Sunday music of mariachis. He raised himself up on an elbow and looked at the clock radio, empty of time and black where the hour and minutes usually glowed. But when he turned the knob, the music of Mexican violins and trumpets rose up, followed by a *grito* that hung like an air raid. He sat up and leaned toward the music he had missed all his life because he had lived his life against a bank wall.

That morning, Mrs. Garcia fixed him breakfast—*chorizo con huevos*—and they ate, he and Roberto, while Mrs. Garcia kept the tortillas coming. They ate on the patio where Gus intended to sit sometimes, but not always, to sit by himself and speak to his legs, those mules, those trusty mules that had carried him through so many eventless years.